CIVILIAN

CIVILIAN

A Novel

Anthony J. Sirico

*PETER
THANK YOU — HOPE YOU
ENJOY THE STORY!*

iUniverse, Inc.
New York Lincoln Shanghai

Civilian

iUniverse books may be ordered through booksellers or by contacting:

iUniverse
2021 Pine Lake Road, Suite 100
Lincoln, NE 68512
www.iuniverse.com
1-800-Authors (1-800-288-4677)

Because of the dynamic nature of the Internet, any Web addresses or links contained in this book may have changed since publication and may no longer be valid.

This is a work of fiction. All of the characters, names, incidents, organizations, and dialogue in this novel are either the products of the author's imagination or are used fictitiously.

ISBN: 978-0-595-42464-1 (pbk)
ISBN: 978-0-595-86798-1 (ebk)

Printed in the United States of America

Thank you to Sue Gould for putting my thoughts on paper
and to September and Kathryn Sirico for making it a reality.
Special thanks also to: Jennie Bedusa, Gaila Perran, Sandra Melzer, and Marcia
Nishball.

CHAPTER 1

I stroked the gleaming blade of my knife tenderly as I wrapped it back up in an old handkerchief. It had to be put back into its usual safe hiding place in the bottom drawer of my bureau when I heard the stirring of my mother and father outside my bedroom door. I had risen early that morning, as I do most mornings. However, I knew this day would be a bit different from the others.

Looking back, I was thirteen years old, and this was my first day back to school, following a long hot summer in my predominantly Italian neighborhood. The season was changing, and I knew I would miss the wonderful late afternoon aromas of fresh pizza baking in the brick oven in my back yard. My grandmother and grandfather lived upstairs in our two-family house, allowing my parents and I to live on the first floor. My grandfather was a baker, and so it was in our backyard that the family would gather for lively conversations and great dishes of food—always a lot of food—fresh fruits, cheeses and breads.

My time for long solitary bike rides, where I could daydream and thoroughly enjoy my own company for hours at a time, while leaving my neighborhood behind, would soon be over. Other areas intrigued me. I liked seeing how others lived in large, sprawling homes with manicured lawns, in contrast to the smaller working class houses in my own neatly kept neighborhood.

Summer's end also meant there would be little time to use my trusty throwing knife in target practice out behind the garage. I was actually becoming quite accurate with my aim, and I took great delight as the knife left my hand and found itself directly in the center of my handmade wooden target. The knife was a gift, the year before, from my grandfather, and I cherished it as my greatest treasure.

The target and the knife, however, were a secret between my grandfather, or "Papa," and me. My mother would have been fearful and would never have approved.

Even when I was a small boy, I admired and was fascinated by the Stiletto that my grandfather always carried with him. When he gave the knife to me, he warned, in his heavy Italian accent: "Always have control of the weapon, son; treat it with great respect, and never use it to harm … unless of course you want to get rid of your grandmother's cats!" he added with a wink and a smile.

My lingering thoughts of summer and freedom were behind me now as I made my way into the kitchen. My mother gave me an approving glance as she pushed my juice and cereal bowl toward me.

"You have a good day and be a good boy," she said as she gave me—her only son—a warm hug, sending me out the back door with my lunch box and school bag. My father had left the house early in the morning to take the bus into town for work at the factory. My father worked hard to provide for our small family and missed out on so many family events.

As my mother cleaned up the kitchen, I know she thought of me. She believed in her heart that I was different from the other boys in the neighborhood. I was the quiet type, keeping mostly to myself. My friends consisted of just a few kids from the neighborhood that I had grown up with since childhood.

I walked quickly to catch up with my friends, as they waited for me by the corner, for the short walk to school. This would be the start of my first year of high school at St. Anthony's. I was definitely a willing student, but had to struggle, putting in many hours of study to maintain my B average. Motivation for me was in looking forward to an even more promising soccer season than the previous year. Soccer was the great passion of my life. True, I was a bit smaller in stature than my friends, but my strong legs, quickness and agility made me a success on the school soccer team.

My neighborhood had buzzed all summer with stories of Mario, our neighborhood's new boy from Italy. I met Mario early in June, practicing soccer. He was dynamic when it came to playing the game. He had been playing in Italy since he was old enough to walk and, boy, did it show. The boys were in awe. Since I had always been the star of the team, I knew I could learn a lot from Mario. Over the summer, we played one-on-one for hours at a time, and I felt comfortable that this would be my best soccer season ever.

CHAPTER 2

The first few weeks of school flew by, and before long, it was time for the first official soccer practice with the coach. Of course, the players had been practicing on their own almost every day after school and on Saturday afternoons. Soccer was the most popular sport in the Italian neighborhood, and the town was proud of our team's undefeated record. Since the 6th Grade, the coach realized what a gem he had in me, and soon had me teaching the team how to use the ball in complicated maneuvers with skill. With myself playing forward, and Mario playing center, we were an unstoppable team. Word spread quickly, and our team soon had strong neighborhood support. It was no longer a game for just the parents and players.

Each week, games were played against the other area schools, and our team from St. Anthony's was soon on its way to being undefeated. We all came alive with enthusiasm as we took our places on the field. We were covered in sweat as our young strong legs carried us up and down the field, passing one to another with careful precision. No doubt, we were a great delight to watch even for those townsfolk who did not understand the ins and outs of the game. My mother and grandfather made it to all my games—watching quietly from the side as I raced toward the goal with lightning speed, adding yet more goals to the usually lopsided scores.

The neighborhood people who came to the games included well-dressed men from the private Italian Club. They were mainly older men—with the exception of one, a big muscular young man in his late teens. He always shouted words of encouragement to the team, loudly cheering us on.

After one hard fought game, he came over to me and slapped me on the back. "You got a good thing going for you here, Johnny. What's your secret?"

"I dunno; I just love the game. It's hard work, but it's worth it to me," I said.

"I like your commitment; we need more people like you," the young man continued. "Keep it up. You're gonna go far. We'll keep in touch. My name is Nick."

Nick was a real neighborhood guy. He had quit school a while back and had been in trouble with the police from time to time—mainly just for scrap fighting. Nick had come from a broken home. His mother was an alcoholic and his father had been shot and killed when Nick was just a boy. At a young age, he took pride in hanging out with what was known as "wiseguys". The only commitment he had to himself was the time he spent at the gym working out.

I felt flattered that Nick went out of his way to talk to me. I figured he must have money, since his clothes were stylish and his black shoes were always perfectly polished. I wondered what Nick did for a living, especially since he looked like he was just out of high school. I watched as the men from the club climbed back into their long, shiny, black car.

"Never you mind!" my mother said, when I asked about Nick later that night at home.

"You don't need to know what they do; it's not for you, John," my father chimed in without looking up from reading the newspaper. That put an end to my questions for the night, but did not end my curiosity.

This conversation with my parents made me even more curious about the men, Nick in particular. I brought up the subject of the well-dressed men to some of the other players on my soccer team. They let me in on the secret information that my parents were keeping from me.

They explained to me that the men from the club were mainly small time racketeers involved in the world of gambling, loan sharking, booking numbers and fencing—not to mention roughing people up when debts were not paid on time. These words were all foreign to me. I found it hard to believe that Nick, who seemed so nice and polite, would do something like that for a living.

"It would be so neat to do something like that, wouldn't it?" Mario asked after hearing about the glorified life of crime and corruption. "Look how much money they must have and how well they probably live—not to mention the excitement of going to work each day. I bet they never know what to expect," he said as we were walking into an empty field to kick the ball around. "Look at the way Nick dresses and how much respect he probably gets from people," Mario added.

"Sounds like people could have more of a fear of him than respect," I replied. I knew Nick's way of life would never be suitable for me. I already knew I wanted more from my life than my hard working, but unskilled, father could ever provide for me, but I also knew I had to go about it in the right way. My mother and father had instilled these values in me at a very young age. I wanted to be educated and to then find a quiet and comfortable life—a life that was not complicated. This, I thought, would make me happy.

As we reached the field to play soccer, we were met by a handful of older boys from the neighborhood who had also gone to the field to kick the ball around. In the middle of playing, I saw my dog, who had wandered from home, coming toward me. I tried to get rid of him on the sidelines, but Blackie wanted to be more than just a bystander. He chased the ball as it was kicked from player to player. One of the older boys almost tripped over the dog. He became angry and started cursing.

"Somebody get this goddamn dog out of here," he yelled as he ran over to Blackie and gave him a swift kick to his side.

I ran over to my dog faster than anyone had ever seen me run. I jumped the boy and beat my fists into his face. I was going for the kid's throat when the other boys, who were amazed by my reaction, tore the two of us apart. It took more than three boys to get me off the other boy, leaving the boy scraped, bruised and bleeding. I felt a rage inside of me that day that I had never shown nor felt before. Shaking and sobbing, I picked up Blackie and carried him home.

The "Blackie" incident was the only one that marred an otherwise exciting and victorious season for me. After settling into school and my studies, I began delivering the newspaper after soccer practice. I raced my bike along my paper route, tossing the papers into driveways, always trying to set a record time delivering to fifty-two neighborhood families before darkness came. I would sometimes see Nick and his buddies on the street, going in and out of local restaurants. Nick always shouted a big hello to me and gave me a big wave. Nick's overtures of friendliness continued to surprise and flatter me in some strange way.

CHAPTER 3

Later on in the school year, I learned that a scout from St. Lawrence Prep School had been keeping an eye on me all season. I was awarded, for my excellence in soccer, a scholarship for the following year at St. Lawrence. As much as I disliked the thought of leaving on a train every morning, for the forty-five minute commute to Prep, I agreed with my mother and father that it was an opportunity too good to pass up. By the spring of my freshman year, it was agreed that I would be leaving my few close buddies behind. Mario and the others were not happy to learn of my decision, as they knew they would be losing their star soccer teammate and a true and loyal friend. They all knew that it would not be the same without Mario and me as the forceful duo controlling the outcome of the soccer games.

Yes, my teammates were going to miss me and, apparently, so would one girl from my Latin class. She had noticed me due to all the attention focused on my athletic scholarship and, without any provocation from me, had developed a crush on me. I found out about the girl's crush in a less than pleasant way. On a Sunday morning, I was on my way to the church to serve at the 10:00 a.m. Sunday Mass. This was the "cool" Mass that teenagers and many adults preferred in comparison to the 8 a.m. attended by the grammar school kids and families. Along the way to church, I caught up with a couple of my buddies. They told me that a kid from school was looking for me because his girlfriend had a crush on me. She had been admiring me, and this made him jealous and angry. My friends alerted me that the boy was going to confront me after Mass. I assisted two other altar boys with preparing the altar, and throughout the Mass I was praying that it would never end. I hated confrontation. When the Mass ended, I cautiously left the altar boys' dressing room behind the sacristy from the rear side exit, hoping not to be spotted. The kid was there, in the shadows, waiting for me. He was snarling that I should "stay away" from his girl. When I tried to explain that I had no interest in her, and that I would soon be transferring to another school, he still didn't cool off. A small crowd of high school kids gathered, and as if he hadn't heard a word I said, the boy began pushing me, trying to knock me down. One push led to a shove, and before I knew it, we were in a full-fledged fight—and I was losing! Thank God, Nick had been at the same Mass, and as he was making his way out of the church, he heard the commotion. He strolled over to the group of kids, asked what the problem was and settled the dispute *his* way. Stronger than both the other kid and myself put together, Nick easily lifted him right off the ground and slammed him up against the stone church building. Nick warned the boy that if he had dealings with me, he would have to deal with him as well, and told the kid to get the hell outta there. Nick said he better not ever again see anyone trying to mess me up. There were no further incidents of hostility towards me, either because no one else had an issue with me, or—more likely, because everyone was so impressed with Nick and feared his temper.

Freshman year passed quickly and, before I knew it, I was once again putting another summer behind me. I spent a few of my last days before school, riding my bike to the beach. I ran into Nick at the beach one day and told him of my scholarship to Prep in the Fall.

Nick asked, "Do you think you belong there?"

"I dunno," I said. "I just know that I need to give it a shot."

"Go for it then," said Nick, and promised he would come and watch me play soccer that fall.

My daily commute to St. Lawrence began. I felt lonely. I also knew that when soccer season began, a lot would be expected of me. It didn't take long to figure out my own teammates were trying to ignore me on the soccer field during practice, rarely kicking the ball to me, keeping it amongst themselves. The coach quickly stepped in.

Before long, I proved to all of them that my presence on the field was valuable, and the rest of the team soon fell into place. I became a dominant member of the team. Once the starting whistle blew, I somehow managed to be everywhere I needed to be. Soon the boys who ignored me in the hallways, were becoming my best buddies on the field.

Nick was on the sidelines during one of my home games. I was so happy to see a familiar face cheering me on! Unfortunately, my mother and grandfather were unable to make it to all the games, due to the distance between our home and the competitions.

The boys on the bench also noticed my well-dressed friend. Nick's slicked back hair glistened in the sunlight. The boys made comments about who this man might be.

"I smell garlic," snickered one of the boys, when I ran over to Nick after the game.

"I told you I would come and see ya, Johnny."

"I'm so glad you did. I miss having faces that I know in the crowd," I told him.

"Is that all you miss?" Nick asked.

"Actually, I miss my old school, and I miss my buddies. I miss just about everything from my old life."

"So, do you feel like you belong here? Do you feel comfortable?" pressed Nick.

"No. I don't feel comfortable at all. I don't dress like these guys here, and I don't have the money to throw around like they do. I don't feel like I belong here—except for soccer, and that's almost over."

"You need to do what is comfortable for you, Johnny; it's never wrong."

I nodded and felt sad as I left Nick to go into the locker room.

"Hey," Nick called after me, "how 'bout meeting me this Saturday for some skeet shooting? I'll meet you at noon at the corner of Cedar and Main. We'll have you cheered up in no time!"

This last exchange put a smile on my face and a bounce in my step as I nodded to Nick that I would be there.

I hurried through my chores on Saturday morning and told my mother I was going for a bike ride. I didn't dare say I was going to meet Nick. My mother would not have understood, and would never have approved of the relationship I had with this new friend.

"We're goin' to the Gun Club. Get in!" said Nick, while jumping out of his big car to put my bike in the trunk.

"Have you ever fired a shotgun?" Nick asked, as we drove through town.

"No, never," I answered. "Actually, I've never even seen a real gun up close."

As we walked through the Gun Club, my eyes were everywhere. I had never seen anything like this. Most of the men were standing with their shotguns at their shoulders. The older men just grunted and nodded their heads as I followed Nick to our station.

"You watch first," Nick cautioned, as he loaded his shotgun. "This is a Brownie Under and Over," Nick explained as he lifted the gun and began firing.

I was fascinated just watching the accuracy of Nick's aim each time he shot. It was soon my turn, and I was surprised at how comfortable the shotgun felt on my shoulder. I pulled the trigger and felt the kickback as the first clay pigeon exploded. Over and over, I fired, enjoying myself tremendously. It was obvious that my hand-eye coordination proved to be a great asset for me. Nick watched patiently as I moved from one section to the next, totally focused on my targets. I hit nineteen out of twenty-five for my first round. Nick told me to continue with another round, and I blasted twenty-two out of twenty-five targets. The men around me turned their heads towards me, hearing Nick loudly praising me.

"Your score beats most of the guys that come here all the time," Nick said, while placing his hands on my shoulder. We went inside the club for something to drink and were joined by two other men. The men ordered beer, while I had a hot chocolate. I couldn't help but notice that the two men had small guns on their hips. Much to my surprise, I did not feel uneasy about their guns; I actually felt more grown up and just a little cocky.

The men asked me how I liked the skeet shooting. I told them that it was my first time and that it was great. I told them how I liked the feel of it and even the sound.

"A gun is powerful," one of the men said. "It makes you judge and jury."

"I'm glad that you like it," said Nick. "Next time, we'll go down to Winchester. There you can shoot a 22 Winchester Rifle at the range. I think you will really like the feel of that in your hands."

A few Saturdays later, I met Nick again, this time at the Italian Club. I told my mother I was meeting up with some school friends at the park. Deep down, I felt bad about the lies to her, but if my mother had known where I wanted to go, my going would have been forbidden. I had no choice but to lie. She viewed Nick and his friends as gangsters. Guns were never even discussed at our house, much less seen and handled. Yet, I felt compelled to go with Nick, and I wasn't even sure why. Maybe it was like having my secret knife. No one except my grandfather knew of the knife's existence, and I derived great pleasure from having it. I certainly did not know Nick well, but I was intrigued by him. Nick was someone totally unlike anyone I had ever known before. I felt safe with him.

During the ride down to Winchester, Nick asked me how school was going. I said I was still unhappy there, especially now that soccer was over. I was keeping up a good front to my friends and family, not wanting to let my mother and father down. They were so proud of their only son attending such a great prep school, but I knew I had to talk to them over the holidays if I were still feeling the same way.

When we arrived at Winchester's, I was surprised to see how dark it was inside. Only the targets off in the distance were lighted, and the long aisles were divided into cubbies. Nick paid the fees for me and handed me a rifle.

"Come on, I'll show you how to load it and hold it. Watch me," Nick said.

I watched as Nick shot off his rounds and pulled his target in on the long pulley. "Not bad," Nick said as he examined all the holes in the center of the paper. "Your turn now, Johnny. Stand free and rest your arms on the holder."

I did as Nick said and began shooting. After the first round, they pulled my target in and they could not believe what they saw. The small bull's eye was completely gone. I reloaded and shot another round.

Nick was so impressed with my accuracy, he said, "Geez, you don't need me anymore; you're a natural!"

After that day, I tried to earn as much money as I could by cleaning garages for my neighbors and by finding and returning soda bottles, so I could spend more time on weekends going to Winchester's to shoot with Nick. Nick always seemed to have plenty of money, but it was important for me to pay my own way. I looked forward to my Saturday afternoons with Nick and with his friends who joined us. These excursions made my life bearable until I was able to speak to my parents about my being unhappy at school.

During my Thanksgiving break, I sat my parents down and explained to them how unhappy I was at Prep.

"I've tried, but I'm just not fitting in," I told them.

My mother rose with tears in her eyes, "Why, John, we had no idea you were the least bit unhappy. Why do you keep things like this inside of you? Of course you'll come back as soon as we can make the arrangements."

I felt such a relief that they were so understanding. I had been so afraid of appearing to be a failure in their eyes.

My old friends and I got together at the annual Thanksgiving Day football game. Mario was one of the first guys I saw as I approached the old group. Mario told me how much I was missed during the soccer season. All the guys were happy to hear of my decision to come back to our old school for the second semester. I was thrilled to be going back to St. Anthony's to finish my sophomore year.

As my friends and I were involved in our activities and in our day-to-day projects and assignments, the world around us was changing. It was the mid-60s, the time when the Vietnam War, protests, and young men heading off to fight a war in a distant land, were the major topics of conversation everywhere.

My family and I were very much aware of the war and the affect it was having on our neighborhood families and their sons. The young men who enlisted, or who were drafted, were from primarily blue collar neighborhoods and rural areas of the country. Very few of these eighteen-year-olds really knew what was happening outside of their own surroundings—much less what was really happening in Vietnam on the other side of the globe. Most did not know why the United States was involved, nor why their boys were being sent to fight the war. But, they had been raised to trust their government's judgment and to be patriotic. They believed it was for the good of their country, and that they must leave home and defend the backbone of democracy. This war was no more real to my family and friends than a program on our television sets. The lack of true understanding was not due to any particular ignorance; any war is never fully understood until years later when it is dissected by historians, if even then.

In my neighborhood, the war became the most talked about topic during social gatherings, especially when each month, local boys' lives were touched and changed forever. It was accepted that it was America's mission to stop the spread of Communism. The people of South Vietnam needed our help to stop the aggression of the Communist North Vietnamese. It was the duty of the U.S. to step in and aid an otherwise helpless country in defending itself. Or, at least, that is what people were led to believe.

One season followed the next, and time passed quickly for me. Before I knew it, I was in my senior year of high school. Returning to my old school was the right decision. I was once again comfortable with myself and with the familiarity of my classmates, family and neighborhood.

CHAPTER 4

After delivering the papers one bitter cold winter day, I was hurrying home on my bike at dusk, when I took a short-cut through a narrow alley. As I entered the alley, I saw someone up ahead being held from behind by a large person. As I got closer, I saw that it was Nick being held by one guy and roughed up by another. As I approached the assault, I froze. Then, I slipped quickly from my bike and grabbed a glass Coke bottle from the side of the alley. In one motion, I flung the bottle towards the large shadow of the aggressor. The bottle caught him on the temple, dropping him to his knees. The other guy dropped Nick, and both men ran off, one helping the other. I rushed over to Nick, who was hunched over on the ground, holding his stomach.

"Where is the bag?" groaned Nick. "Where's the bag? I gotta get the money!"

I felt around the ground and found a small but heavy paper bag. "This must be what you're looking for," I said, helping Nick to his feet. I walked him out of the alley to the lighted sidewalk.

"Are you okay?" I asked.

"Yeah, I'll be fine ... especially since they didn't get the money from me, thanks to you, Johnny. This is just part of my job."

I could never understand why Nick did what he did. It seemed so dumb to risk your life just to have flashy clothes and lots of money to throw around.

"You come back to the club with me, Johnny, while I report this to my boss. I want to thank you, and I know the guys will want to thank you, too."

"I gotta get home," I said. "Since you're okay, I'm leaving."

Nick called to me as I was getting back on my bike, "I owe you one, Johnny!"

I called back, "No, we're even now! Remember the church?"

The next time I saw Nick was at the Italian Club, a few Saturdays later. Though I never asked about it, Nick wanted to talk to me about the business he was in.

"I'm just a small fish here in a big pond. The bigger bosses own the pinball and vending machines throughout the local towns and The City. Lots of cash changes hands, and lots of pressure is on store owners who don't cooperate with the boss's way of doing things. It was my own fault that I was pushed over the other day. I should have been prepared for something like that happening. I'm young, but I'm a good learner. So are you, Johnny. Keep what I am telling you to yourself. The Mob is big, but if you treat it fair, it will treat you fair. I'm not a *civilian*, Johnny; I'm a small part of an organization that does things its own way.

I listened and nodded, but I knew what Nick and his buddies were doing was wrong. I knew I could never live my life as they did.

                     *   *   *   *

Still in my senior year, I fell in love. It felt as if a heavy curtain had been lifted and daylight streamed into my life—as if I were opening my eyes for the first time. She would look up and smile at me as I took my seat in history class. I could feel my face catch on fire. She was so beautiful! Her long, shiny dark hair and her perfect oval face attracted every bit of my attention, overwhelming me and leaving me speechless. Each day, as class ended, I tried to think of something to say to her, but the words never came out of my mouth.

One day in class, a note was passed to me. It read: "Wait for me after class. Elizabeth." The rest of that class was a blur, and as I got up to leave when class ended, my book and class notes fell off the desk and dropped onto the floor. The kids around me laughed as I went scrambling on my knees to retrieve my papers. My face was hot as I thought: "I'm such a jerk! How can I go talk to her now?"

She was standing just outside the door as I rushed out of the classroom. I felt as if my body and my life were in slow motion as I approached her. I managed a weak, "Hi."

The smile that she gave me illuminated her face and I could only think: "God, she is so pretty. She's so pretty." I couldn't take my eyes off her face.

"I was wondering if you would like to go to the Turn About Twirl Dance with me?" she asked.

I stammered, "Ahh, yeah, sure," after what seemed like five hours to get the words out of my mouth.

"Great," she said. "Later we can talk about the details."

She turned and walked away with girl friends who had been waiting for her across the hall.

My feet only skimmed the top step of the school stairs as I ran out of the building to go home that day. I made it home faster than I ever had before, my feet never touching the ground as I passed everyone along the way.

The words came out a little easier each day after class when she would wait for me. I had never looked forward to going to history class as I did now.

The night of the dance quickly approached, and I was so nervous I could hardly contain myself. The dance was crowded as we made our way through the transformed gym. All of our friends were gathering in small circles, Elizabeth and I had eyes only for each other. While others mingled, we danced every dance. I could not believe how fresh and sweet the scent of her skin was as I held her close that night.

This was the beginning of our relationship. We soon spent all of our spare time together. As a seventeen year old boy, I was feeling that my life was quite complete.

Senior year was a busy year for me and all of my buddies. College acceptances were coming in, and some of my friends were going downtown to the recruiter's office to sign up for the Service. The war was raging now, and rather than waiting to be drafted, some felt it was their patriotic duty to enlist.

My relationship with Elizabeth was flourishing, and we spent countless hours side-by-side doing homework, walking, and talking about our futures. It was during one of those long walks that I confided to Elizabeth what had been on my mind.

"I've been giving this a lot of thought," I said, "and I've been wanting to hear how you feel about it. I have not spoken these words out loud yet, not even to my parents. But, I hope you'll hear me out and try to understand what I'm saying."

Elizabeth nodded acceptingly and said softly, "Please tell me what it is you're thinking about, John. It must be something important. I've noticed you've been quiet lately. I haven't asked why because I knew you would tell me when you were ready."

Hesitantly, I began. "I know we have our futures pretty well mapped out, and it all seems smooth and easy. I understand how important our education is. We both want the same things; we both want to be teachers, reaching our goals together. Most importantly, we want to stay together and live a better and more comfortable life than our parents."

Elizabeth reached for my hand as I continued. "But, I feel there is one thing I need to do before I can begin to deal with the future. It's something I need to do now, for me, for us, for our country. I want to enlist in the Service and do my part. I just won't feel whole as a person until I have completed this part of my life. When my two years are up, then I can focus on the rest of my life."

I searched Elizabeth's face for anger or disappointment. She held onto my hand and said, "I want what you want, John. I know you could be deferred for the Army because you would be in school full time, studying to be a teacher. In four years, the war could be over, and you would never have to deal with leaving here and fighting. It would be selfish of me, though, to keep you all to myself. Even if it means being apart physically, we will continue to grow together. We need to be whole people to face the future together. We need to always back each other, and I know we'll be stronger for it."

I felt relieved. We held onto each other for a long time. We both felt our love become even stronger. Together, we told my parents and grandparents about my decision. I had to repeatedly assure my hysterical mother and grandmother that I would return unharmed and safe. "I may be one of the ones that do not even go to Vietnam," I explained to them, "but it will be okay if I do go because I will survive."

CHAPTER 5

That spring of 1967, things seemed different to me as the chapter of my high school life was coming to a close. The grass never seemed so green; even the buds on the trees somehow seemed brighter and more splendid. Graduation in June was bittersweet. It was, indeed, a joyful time—a time of high spirits, yearbook signings, hugs and handshakes, as the high school class reluctantly, yet optimistically, went about their departures from the safe and secure life they had always known.

Upon receiving my Physical Notice a few weeks following graduation, I went downtown to the Marine Recruiting Office and signed up. My parents, grandparents and Elizabeth were still anxious and concerned, but there was no doubt in my mind that I was making the right decision. I easily passed the physical examination and was notified I would depart for Paris Island, South Carolina, in just six weeks.

A few days after completing my physical, I went downtown to the Club to see Nick. I had been so involved in my day-to-day activities at home, I had not had the time to see my friend. Nick had never called nor approached me at home. It was always up to me to contact him. I was worried about Nick. I had read in the newspaper, only a few days before, that the club where Nick hung out had been raided for booking and stolen furs. I had read that a court date had been set. I was relieved to find Nick at the Club and we sat down together to catch up on each other's news. Nick told me only a few men, including him, had been arrested.

"It's no big deal," Nick told me. "I will do, at most, six months to a year. I can still work from within. This is just a small price to pay. Besides, the rewards far outweigh the penalty inflicted on me. So, tell me about yourself, John. What have you been up to? It's been a while since I've seen or heard from you."

Over coffee, I brought Nick up to date on all that was happening in my life, including my relationship with Elizabeth and my decision to enter the Service.

"Geez, I was counting on helping you get out of the service when the time came. Here you go and sign up for the Marines! I shoulda talked to ya sooner, Johnny."

"It wouldn't have mattered," I told him. "I need to go. It's something I have to do."

Nick tried to explain to me how corrupt the world is: the politicians, the Catholic Church, the country, everything.

"What you see, John, and what you are told is not the way it is. Don't believe everything you're told. You're just another head for them to brainwash. Follow your gut to survive and you will always come through. You may need favors from certain people someday, even though you may not believe in what they do. You are still so innocent. Ah, you will learn these things for yourself. I will always be here for you, John, no matter where or what. Someday you just may need a favor," Nick said with a friendly smirk.

Nick gave me a warm embrace as we got up to leave.

"Hey, Johnny," Nick called as I was heading for the door, "I guess neither one of us is a civilian anymore. Good luck!" I felt a chill as I left the club.

＊　　　＊　　　＊　　　＊

Weeks flew by as I prepared to leave home. I pushed myself in training to be in my best physical shape. I lifted weights and ran more miles every day. At the time, I was also working at the local supermarket as a stock boy. Elizabeth and I spent as much time together as we could. We both knew that the road ahead of us would be challenging, yet we shared the same belief that we would someday be together again.

A few days before my departure, Elizabeth and I escaped for a whole day. I borrowed a friend's car and we drove far into the countryside. We shared a simple picnic lunch that my mother had prepared. It was a glorious summer day—one that we both would remember and look back on in the days and months to come.

There we were … just the two of us … for the first time completely alone. I had not had very many opportunities to be totally alone with Elizabeth, as everywhere we went, and involved with everything we did, there were always other people around. As if on a mission to find privacy, we discovered a special clearing among the trees, providing us just the right amount of sunlight filtered through the branches of ancient oak trees. We were surrounded by full grown leafy shrubs, as if Mother Nature had created this spot on Earth just for us. Not a soul in the world would see us here. Our picnic lunch was tempting us to sit down and eat, but our picnic blanket was far more inviting. We had been high school sweethearts for only one year, and of course had had some sexual exploratory sessions with one another, but this was the first time that we actually had the freedom and the privacy to even speak of going "all the way" with one another. Beyond our usual hugging and kissing on this day, we instinctively seemed to know what more to do and almost ceremoniously began experimenting with ways to lovingly please and excite one another. We took each other's hands and sat down together, and almost shyly began speaking softly to one another, expressing our love and our desire—as if every word were a secret between us. Our arms found their way around us and encircled us with a bit of a nudge to lie down together. I believe we both experienced an instant and complete feeling of freedom and relaxation—as if every weight ever carried had now been dropped. Snuggling up to one another, tenderly kissing and gently exploring our learned sensitive areas through our clothing, we soon became like two ignited sparklers. The summer sun was no match for the heated passion between us. As we undressed one another, I marveled at her beauty, her softness, her complete acceptance of my overtures, and was amazed by how my slightest touch created such a wanton desire in her. She wanted to give herself to me totally, completely, without reservation, and said so. What more could I have dreamed of? My excitement was urging me to hurry on, but I realized that we might not have such a chance again with one another for a long, long time. I wanted her passion and her joy in our first complete sexual experience to last as long as possible, so I held myself back a bit and attempted to return to a more normal rate of breathing. Elizabeth pushed me over and rolled upon me. She straddled me with her knees, and leaning forward, offered her breasts to my lips—first one, then the other. Barely resting her aroused body on top of mine, she gently swayed herself in random directions until I could no longer control my desire to enter her. I pushed her back down onto our blanket and—with one more look into her eyes for the silent message to continue—I very carefully and slowly eased myself into her. She whispered that I should not move, and so, in this most simple, physical union of our bodies, we each winced with pent up momentum and together felt and released a long and throbbing climax. Never, since that first time with Elizabeth, has sex ever been quite as sweet, pure and thoroughly joyous.

We actually did eat our picnic lunch, smiling and smirking as if we alone had discovered the world's greatest form of communication. As the afternoon drew to a close, we drove back home to where the whole family had gathered together that last Sunday for my farewell dinner. My mother prepared all of my favorite foods, and my grandmother did her best to see that I ate everything. My grandfather took me aside and told me: "You bring your knife with you, John. Keep it with you always. You know how to use it, and I'll sleep better at night knowing it is always with you." My grandfather's eyes filled with tears, and he gave me, his only grandson, a loving hug.

A few days later, hugs, tears and kisses were given freely while I told my mother, father and grandparents goodbye. Elizabeth went to the bus station with me, and we clung on to each other until it was time for me to board the bus. I brushed Elizabeth's tears away, kissed her one more time, and turned to get my new life underway.

I was not alone. At least ten other local guys left that morning with me for a twelve-hour bus ride to South Carolina. Glancing out the window of the bus as it pulled away from the curb, I caught my last glimpse of Elizabeth. She was standing alone on the sidewalk, and I longed to be back there beside her. Soon, however, I found myself half-listening to the many conversations going on around me. The voices droned on as my thoughts turned inward. In my mind, I was trying to put my past behind me and I was looking forward to my unknown future. I was as physically ready as I could be and was now working on mental preparation. Leaving Elizabeth behind did not make this easy.

CHAPTER 6

Upon arrival at Paris Island, and after the initial chaos of checking in and being issued fatigues, I was shown to my bunk. My first meal was in the Mess Hall, with hundreds of other guys my age. The booming voices of the sergeants never let up. When one sergeant finished barking an order, another would take his place. I soon overcame my fears and settled into the discipline and the structure of each day. I knew they were instilling pride in each of us—the special pride that came from being a Marine. It was this pride that would stay with us for the rest of our lives. We were pushed to our limits each day—both physically and mentally. Each day was followed with another day of new, difficult challenges. It was drilled into us that, when faced with the ultimate challenge, it would take more than physical strength alone to conquer it.

I took to my new life as though I had never had another one. I used every ounce of courage and self-discipline I had in me. I consistently turned in the best ranking unit competition scores. I ran. I marched. I swam. I climbed, and I loved every minute of it. I was pushed all the way to the limits that transcend me into another state of mind. This "transcending" was just a part of my personality that had been known to surface at times of great physical or emotional stress. This inner personal drive had surfaced in the past, during my soccer years. It was a part of me that came out when life around me seemed threatening, or when I wanted to overcome a personal inner challenge.

My determination and leadership qualities did not go unnoticed. The sergeants liked what they saw in me. They hand-picked me to wrestle, on the mats, the biggest recruit in the unit and wanted me to push him to his limit. As I struggled with my huge opponent, I brought up that feeling from back on the day my dog was kicked on the soccer field. The rage surfaced, and I held my own with the big guy. When the sergeant finally stopped the wrestling match, the big recruit slapped me on the back and said, "I never expected you to be so fast and strong. Fighting you was like fighting an empty shirt."

At times, when the sergeants walked into the barracks and began screaming at the recruits and getting in our faces, I would run around like the rest of the recruits—touching everything that might be under scrutiny—none of us understanding a word of the foul, loud southern accents.

I enjoyed rifle shooting. It was easy for me and I was near perfect every time. The sergeant asked me where I had learned to shoot, and I just smiled inside and said, "In the Marines, Sir!"

Late one afternoon, in a rare hour of personal time, I found myself behind the barracks, throwing my knife into a plank of wood with paper targets I had found. The pinging noise was heard by the sergeant as he was passing by. He discovered me there and watched as I threw the knife with either hand, flipping it overhand and underhand. The sergeant told me: "You're gonna be a leader, John."

The other recruits wondered why I seemed to be enjoying Boot Camp.

For the most part, everyone else was miserable. The only part that I did not like was the brainwashing. Boot Camp was seventy-percent training and thirty-percent brainwashing. The sergeants tried their best to break us down and to make us cry. Only a select few of us would be transformed into killing machines. I was one man that could not cry. A few of the guys became close to me after that, and together we shared our fears and our feelings about our unknown futures.

We all knew what was happening. We were being trained—in a hurry—for Vietnam. We were filled every day with American propaganda about the Cong, the Enemy. We were pushed to our limits because our lives depended on it. We were trained to hate, to shoot on sight, and to survive. Shooting had to become instinctive. We were all aware of the casualties mounting in Vietnam. Each new group of trainees was a little bit more prepared than the previous batch. Training was becoming more stressful and realistic. Meanwhile, we lived on minimal sleep. We knew that at least a year of our lives would be spent on foreign soil, fighting for our lives and for the lives of our buddies. Crucial to us was survival for ourselves on a day-to-day basis. Saving democracy and allowing the people of Vietnam to enjoy freedom was not uppermost on our minds. Nothing would fully prepare us for the life we would be living in a month from now. We would not smell the smells, nor hear the anguish, nor see the frightened children, nor feel the heat and fatigue until we were face-to-face with it.

With that vision in my mind, I prepared to return home for my last visit before being sent to Nam. I looked forward to enjoying my family and Elizabeth. Certainly, everyone would be proud of my development and my unique distinction of being made a sergeant during the closing ceremonies of Boot Camp. This was rare for a new recruit. Everyone knew about my progress and accomplishments during training, since I had kept in close touch through reading and writing letters into the wee hours of the morning. I had phoned in the news about making sergeant, although I usually kept the phone calls infrequent so as to distance and discipline myself from home attachments.

As much as I had enjoyed training and my honored progress, I was ready to return home. I was ready to leave the rifle ranges, the mock Vietnam villages, the little or no sleep, and the haunting thoughts of the enemy waiting for me.

Several guys had offered me a ride home, but they were all pretty much into the bar scene and I knew that there would be lots of stops on the way home. Besides, on the bus I would have some much needed time to be alone with my thoughts. That was the one thing I missed in the military—time to be with just myself. I knew I was changed after what I had just endured. The physical change was evident: my body was in the most fit condition ever, hard as a rock and yet a bit leaner than when I had begun boot camp. But it was my changed mental state that intrigued me the most. I knew that I was not the same person I had been. I was never more certain about my life's direction. I knew I wanted to go to Nam and survive it. I also knew now it wasn't any major sense of patriotic duty that was compelling me to fight. It just felt so right for me. What about it felt so right? I didn't know; I knew only that I had to do it. I knew I had made the right choice in being where I was right now, rather than at home working a job, or sitting in a college class room. Perhaps those things would come later.

I knew I owed it to Elizabeth to explain the person I had become and my fear of what was to come. I could only pray that she would understand and I believed she would because we had been so close and so much in love.

My homecoming would definitely present a frenzied schedule of good times, but I also wanted quiet time and closeness with my family, Elizabeth, and my friends.

While home for this last visit, I wanted to push the reality of war to the back of my mind and savor each moment with those I loved.

I especially looked forward to spending time alone with Elizabeth. We had already planned in our letters that we would spend as much time alone as we possibly could. We wanted to get to know each other again.

First came the lively "Welcome home!" that greeted me at the front door of the house. My eyes lighted on Elizabeth as the door opened. I was pulled into a warm embrace from my mother and father together, followed by my grandparents. I lifted my grandmother off her feet. The living room was filled with family, friends, and neighbors. Everything that I loved about home came rushing back to me: the familiar smells, the food, the conversation, and the laughter. But underlying it all was a sense of quietness and sadness within my family. They did not understand the war or the protests going on around the country. All they knew was that in a few short days, they would be losing their son to a place far away, where he would be fighting and killing—always with the chance of being killed and not coming back. Their fears were unspoken as they listened to me explaining why I was going and assuring them that I would be back. That was one thing that I knew for sure—I would be back.

Elizabeth and I talked all through the night after everyone had gone home. We tried to make up for the time that we had been apart. We filled each other in on what little was left out of the many letters sent back and forth while I was at camp. My body was leaner; my hair was shorter, but I was the same John that held her and stroked her hair and told her that I would come back so we could spend the rest of our lives together. Elizabeth still couldn't help but worry. Her heart told her I would be back, but her mind questioned the likelihood of my being seriously hurt or even killed. She read every day of the reality of the war and the deaths and the names of the dead listed in the newspaper. But this was now, and I was there, and she felt safe.

CHAPTER 7

I found some time to myself the next day and went to the club. It had been restored from the fire. I wanted to see if any of the guys knew how Nick was doing.

A few weeks after I had left for Boot Camp, Nick had his day in court. He got off much easier than some of his associates because it was his first offense. Nick was sentenced to eighteen months in prison, but only had to serve nine months for good behavior. First chance I had at home, I met with Nick's friend, Sonny, at his restaurant.

Silence greeted me as I walked through the front doors to the club. The faces of the guys looking at me showed that they did not recognize me. What they saw was a self-assured, strong and fit young man; not the high school friend of Nick's that they had known.

"Yo! Sonny, it's me, John," I said to the older man sitting at the table. Sonny jumped up and rushed over to shake my hand and gave me a big hug.

"Hey, you did it! You really did join the Marines. It would be great, Johnny, at any other time, but you know what this god-damned war is all about, don't you? Power and Money!"

I smiled and said, "That's what war is *always* all about: Power and Money."

"Well, you look terrific, Johnny. So, this what-ever-you're-doing agrees with you. You look in great shape.

I said, "Yeah, if you want to get in good shape, I can tell you where to go for a while ... You'll get rid of that gut in no time."

"Fuck you. I'd have to give up all my good meals and bad habits and I ain't doin' that. Come on, have an espresso with me," Sonny said, waving at the guys already at the table to move. "My friend and I are having a talk," he told them.

"Gimme two espressos and a bottle of Anisette," Sonny told one of the guys passing by.

"Do you want to eat, John? I've got manicotti and lasagna in the back."

"No thanks," I said. "I've been eating since I got back yesterday, thanks to my mother and grandmother. They think I'm too thin."

We talked about the neighborhood—small talk. Then, I asked Sonny how I could see Nick.

Sonny said, "You're on the list, Johnny, so you can go visit any time. Nick made sure you were on the list, just in case you had a chance to come home and have time to see him. It would mean a lot to him. If you go up, you can sneak him some food: provolone, pepperoni, some salami. The food on the outside is the one thing Nick misses; it would be appreciated."

Sonny slapped my back as he got up to leave. "Hey, when you go fight this war, don't be the good guy. Be the bad guy. Good guys don't last."

The phone rang as I was about to leave the restaurant. The old man from the back came out and told Sonny it was Nick on the phone.

Sonny hollered to me, "Great! John, you get the phone."

So, I went back in and picked up the phone and said, "Hey, Nick!"

There was a pause, and Nick said, "Oh my God, I don't believe it! How the hell you doin', Johnny?"

"I'm doing all right," I said. I told him I wanted to go see him, so we made arrangements for the day and time.

"Hold on, Nick," I said, "Sonny is swaying back and forth here, so I'll put him on. See you soon."

I waved good-bye to the guys at the tables and one shouted, "Hey, John, you come back now—after you do whatever it is you have to do."

I left feeling good that I had had a chance to see Sonny and talk to Nick.

The next morning, I used my father's car to drive him to work earlier than usual.

"Do you remember that guy, Nick, that used to come to my soccer games in high school?" I asked him.

"Yeah," answered my father.

"Well, I'm going to see him today. He's serving some time in prison, and I told him I'd be up today."

"I don't understand you, John. Why would you want to have anything to do with him? He's a hoodlum."

"It seems like that," I answered, "but inside he's a great guy. And, who knows? Maybe this time in prison will turn him around."

"I'm glad you didn't tell your mother where you were going today. She would never understand," he said, as we arrived at the factory. I let my father out and began the two-hour drive to the prison.

As I drove, I thought about how my life had changed in so many ways in such a short time. I was moving from the soccer field to the battlefield! I knew that what I was heading for would be a life-or-death situation—a gamble, a toss of the dice. I would either come back as a living person or in a body bag for my family and Elizabeth to mourn over. The thought of Elizabeth made me smile, and I knew I had to come back for her.

Driving through the prison gates made me shudder. I checked in and waited in a small room for Nick to be brought in. The situation reminded me of Boot Camp with its same discipline; same emptiness in the men's eyes. When Nick came into the room, we embraced each other.

"Let's go outside to talk," said Nick. "God, you're so big, John. You look really built up."

"You look like you've put on some meat yourself," I said.

Nick replied, "I lift weights every day. Not much else to do here. Geez, I think I'm becoming an athlete myself."

We both laughed.

"We're not talking about the future, are we?" asked Nick, after a time of making small talk. "We're both just living in the present. Day by day, just protect yourself, Johnny, like I do here, and we'll both get through this."

"What *is* your future, anyway, Nick? Now can be the time for you to get out of this lifestyle you're in. What lies ahead for you? Looks to me like a future of either jail or death. It might be exciting for you now, but you haven't even been deeply involved yet. It's not that you're a made man already. Before the big trouble happens, now is the time to get out. Don't you want to have a family and friends that you can really trust? I just don't get it."

Nick responded, "There are no guarantees in life, Johnny. This is who I am and you are who you are. Someday, you'll realize what I am involved with. In the past, I've been involved with big fishes in small ponds. But someday, I will be a big fish in a big pond. And someday, you will realize that your way of life and my way of life are very similar. Think about it, Johnny. Wars are about freedom, power, money, and greed. Whether we're in here or outside, we have always been involved in wars just like the government has. When the big powers can't get the job done, they turn to us. We don't deal in red tape. We just get the job done, and someday when you come back, we'll talk more."

As we walked back inside, Nick pointed out an older man, standing within a group of inmates. "That's a powerful man over there, Johnny, and two of the other inmates are some high-powered lawyers, and they're in here for embezzling. So, you can see: everybody's here.

"I'm glad I know a person like you, Johnny, 'cause no matter what, you're someone to trust, and I don't find that very often. It fills the emptiness that a person like me can have. You'll always be my good friend."

I told Nick about Elizabeth, and Nick wrote a phone number on a piece of paper for me.

"I hope she'll never need this," Nick said, "but I'll let them know who she is, and she will be taken care of while you're gone."

I did feel better knowing that Elizabeth would be taken care of in case she needed protection or help while I was away.

As I turned to go, we both had a warm feeling that neither of us had in the past few months. It was as if we had given each other strength.

The rest of my time at home flew by. "I can't believe I'll be in Vietnam in less than 48 hours," I said to my family and Elizabeth as we sat down for our last dinner together. I was taking an early morning bus back to the barracks from where I would be shipped out. There was a quiet sadness that evening. My grandparents were visibly shaken, and my parents were extremely anxious. I tried to put their fears to rest.

"I want all of you to be as positive as I am. I know I'm coming back, so you need to take good care of yourselves while I'm away, so we can all sit around this table in a year. I want to take all of your positive thoughts with me. That will pull me through."

The next morning, after assuring Elizabeth that I would be fine, I gave her the slip of paper with the phone number on it that Nick had given me.

"I will feel good knowing you have this, just in case you need help," I told her.

Elizabeth didn't really approve of my relationship with Nick, but she understood it was important to me, so she tucked it in her pocket and bravely kissed me good-bye, turned, and walked away. I could not see the tears streaming down her face, nor did I see the tears on the faces of my family as I left that morning. I climbed on the bus and shut that part of my life down.

I was about to move from one world to another within a matter of hours. I racked my brain to visualize what I would be getting into. I realized I had to adjust myself mentally from the world of civilians to the reality of war and being a soldier. Keeping an open mind was the best thing I could do. I silently said a little prayer for my family and for myself and then dozed off. I was prepared physically, but I was not prepared emotionally for the combat that was ahead of me.

*   *   *   *

After a long plane trip, we arrived at the Oakland, California base in a flurry of activity like I had never seen. Mass amounts of equipment were being shuttled around in preparation for departure. I was relieved to see my buddies from camp. Everybody had been brought back. I felt more at ease just by talking with them and some of the other guys that would be going with me as well. All the men were fearful of the unknown world they were about to enter. The only thing they had to go by were stories that had made it back home.

Before I knew it, we were on a plane to Tokyo, Japan, where we spent a few days processing papers and being told to hurry up and wait. All of the men were anxious and sleep was hard to come by. This would be the most rest I would be getting for quite some time. I was being sent over as an individual replacement for someone whose tour had ended, and who made it through, and was probably thrilled at the prospect of going home alive.

After the 20-hour flight to Okinawa, the next leg of the trip on a smaller plane to Danang, seemed to pass by in the blink of an eye.

I got off the plane and walked across the tarmac, the intense heat of the sun hitting me like a high fever. The heat had an unidentifiable odor, and it enveloped us with what proved to be the overpowering and repulsive smell of rotting vegetation, filling our nostrils and sickening our stomachs. "Welcome to Nam!"

Gladly, I learned that a guy named Malcolm was to be going with me on my field assignment. I had met Malcolm in Basic, and then again, in advanced training. He was a big burly black man from Detroit. I felt more of a sense of safety with this guy who had been covering his own back all his life, than I would have with somebody from the suburbs who had never experienced violence before. Whether at home, or at war, Malcolm was a survivor. After a few days of paper processing and waiting, I finally received my assignment.

We all boarded buses with wire screens on the windows, to prevent grenades from being thrown in, as we passed through the villages to our destination. I saw no friendly faces among the Vietnamese; only children begging through the streets.

Malcolm, two other guys, and I were dropped off in what seemed to be the middle of the jungle. We were right; we were in the midst of heavy foliage and thick underbrush everywhere. This was where we met up with our Unit.

We were not welcomed with open arms by the men already stationed there. We were called "cherries," and because we were the new recruits, we were not trusted. Nobody wanted to be near a new guy. How a new man reacted under fire was the most important question, as this was not training; this was not pretend. This was life and death. How we reacted under fire in the jungle would determine who went home in a body bag. The new guys were sent to the rear of the Unit to gain experience.

I felt I had to kill right away. I knew if I didn't right at the start, I would not make it home. I didn't have to wait long. The first ambush came quickly, and the gunfire began. Afterwards, it left me feeling sick and weak. As the smoke lingered like a dense fog, there was a sense of calm that filled the air. I could never have been prepared for what I had just done.

This first ambush was a major hurdle for the new recruits. We all vomited uncontrollably when the shooting was over. The platoon leader told us that was a good sign that we would make it. Malcolm tried to make light of our first encounter with death, and he helped to ease the transition with the older troops.

CHAPTER 8

Nick did his time in state prison along with other men who had committed white-collar crimes and quickly learned the ropes: who to know, who to stay away from, and who to buy cigarettes from. He immediately recognized a few people he had dealings with in the past, but settled into his own routine, staying away from all illegal activities going on around him. He kept in touch with friends on the outside and he heard of a lot of changes going on. He learned of territory disputes and power struggles within families. Many egos were being knocked around. He was told, kiddingly, that he was safer right where he was. Word soon got around that a boss from a high family was in a cell a few blocks down from Nick. This guy was a big league player and was from out of state. Nick noticed the large white-haired man repeatedly when they were outside in the exercise yard. Soon, the older boss was asking about Nick.

"Who's the kid?" he asked his cronies. He liked the way that Nick handled himself.

A fellow inmate told Nick that his friend, the white-haired man named Pope, wanted to meet him. It was arranged that Nick was introduced to Pope and learned from him that they had mutual associates on the outside. Nick was impressed with Pope's knowledge. They often played cards and chess with a select group of guys.

Nick was hearing about more and more problems on the outside getting progressively worse. There were some serious changes in power as well as several public killings. Nick was even more dismayed when he learned his old club had been torched. Nick had "gone away" just in time. He wondered how these turf changes would affect the hierarchy of command when he got out.

In conversations with Pope, Nick confided to him his concern about his outside world.

He smiled, "I already know what happened and what is going to happen."

Nick realized his own world of Mafia was much larger than he had ever imagined. Pope told him that if they wanted to reach him in there, they could.

"Don't talk to anyone about anything until things change," Pope advised.

One morning, Nick overheard a conversation between two Mafia wanna-be's in the shower. He learned they were being paid to go after Pope. Initially, Nick didn't know what to do. He got the word to the old man that a plan was in motion to get rid of him. Pope just smiled and thanked Nick for telling him.

Pope's buddies asked him, "What do you want us to do about this?"

The old man answered, "Why should I trust this kid, Nick? He is giving me a message. We'll just keep our eyes open, and you keep an eye on the kid."

At breakfast a few days later, the cafeteria was only half full. Guys were still shuffling in from their cells. Nick was already sitting and eating, when he looked up to see Pope walking in alone, which he frequently did for the early breakfast line shift. Nick watched two guys get up from a table together and walk across the room toward Pope. A noisy fight suddenly erupted from the far side of the room, breaking the early morning quiet. Everyone turned to see what was happening.

Nick thought to himself: "This is it," and leaped up in slow motion. The two thugs were just about on Pope, when Nick dove up and over the last table, knocking the old man to the floor under him. Nick felt the blade to his shoulder before he saw the blood flowing down his arm. The two thugs were held on the floor by other inmates until the guards reached him.

Nick gave his hand to Pope to help him up. The old man smiled up at Nick.

"What the hell are you smiling at?" Nick asked. Blood was pouring out of Nick's shoulder.

"I trust you with my life, Nick. I can trust you with my business. Go get that wound bandaged up and, hey, Nick—thanks."

When Nick's shoulder began to heal, he was permitted back outside in the exercise yard. He began a series of short meetings with the old man each morning. Pope told Nick he wanted him to work for him on the outside. "I'll be here in prison for awhile for tax dealings, but that's no problem for you. I'll be setting you up when you get out. You'll report directly to me. I'm no small potatoes, Nick. You will be doing things you have never dreamed of."

Nick could hardly contain himself. He was so excited. This was an opportunity for him that he never expected. He could hardly imagine working for a Don of this magnitude. As the old man talked, Nick listened and hung on to every word. He learned about the character of the Mob, controlling your outward feelings, not letting anyone know your next move, and how to just blend in.

The old man schooled Nick each day.

Nick asked, "How do you know if everything is okay with your family on the outside? How do you know they're all still behind you with so many changeovers happening?"

Pope smiled and said, "Don't go to the movie Thursday night."

Nick knew something was up, and it had to do with the questions that the old man left unanswered. So he sat in his cell Thursday night and waited for the word. Early the next morning, Nick was informed that the two thugs who tried to stab Pope were found with knives stabbed right through their chairs as they sat and watched the movie. The men were found dead when the lights were turned on.

Time passed quickly, and Nick had only a few weeks left to serve in prison.

Pope gave Nick some advice: "Everybody is going to be your friend. Trust nobody, fear nobody, and get to know everybody." Then, he gave Nick two names to contact and an address.

"They'll be expecting you. They know all about you. Remember our deal is silent. You'll just be one of the boys."

Pope smiled at Nick as they shook hands on the morning of the day Nick was released. Nick felt great strength pass between them as they hugged each other. He loved it when the old man smiled.

Nick felt giddy with freedom as he returned to his hometown to tie up a few loose ends. He was not packing many clothes to take with him, as he knew he needed a new look for his future work. Pope had told him he needed to dress "like you belong to a country club or to the yacht club—understated. I don't want you to stand out. You want to look the part you are playing."

Pope had also told him to cut off his sideburns and to "get the grease out of your hair. The last thing you want to look like is a wise guy. You need to wear a blue blazer, gray slacks and a striped tie. Real straight," he said.

Following Pope's suggestions, Nick had to reinvent his image, starting with clothes shopping. It was a new experience, buying clothes in high end, Ivy League type stores that carried exclusively Italian and English apparel. However, he did not see himself in a blue blazer with brass buttons and gray flannel pants with high pockets, but rather in black cashmere and camel hair sport jackets. Once inside the store, he acclimated easily and went from head to toe, purchasing two and three-piece suits.

After completing his purchases, Nick's next stop was at his old club. He was pleased to see that it was being repaired after it had burned down. The door was open, so he went in and sat down with a few of his old cronies. They had already heard the news that Nick was moving to the city to work for Pope. The word was that Nick was going to be just another guy on payroll: a runner, a thumb breaker, paying his dues at the end of each week. They had no idea about the power Pope had already given to Nick. Neither did Nick.

On the day he was to report, Nick found the address Pope had given him. He reached the club late that afternoon, and the door was opened by some of the guys. The old man had gotten word back that Nick was to be expected and was to receive no special treatment. "He's just another guy I want on the street," Pope had told them.

When Nick walked in, there were six guys sitting around a long table, drinking espresso. They greeted Nick, but they seemed cool and distant.

They don't know me, Nick thought. *I am an outsider right now. I'll have to prove myself. I know I'll be tested like any new kid on the block. Like, how far can you throw a baseball or football?*

Nick told them, "I'm here to do whatever you need me to do. This is not new to me."

A guy that was on the phone hung up and came over to Nick to introduce himself. "I'm Sal. We've been expecting you, Nick. Where you been? Home to see your mother?"

The guys started chuckling. "Yeah, I did go home to see my mother," said Nick.

"That's where you should have gone," said one of the guys. "Don't ever forget your family."

An older gentleman came out from the back room, carrying a tray with an espresso pot on it. He put it on the table and in a quiet voice asked, "Does anyone want more?"

Several of the guys said yes to him. "I will get another cup," he said, looking in Nick's direction.

Nick said, "I'll get it. Where are the cups?"

The man replied, "Finally, someone here has courtesy and manners. Come with me and I'll show you where they are."

Nick followed him to the back room and introduced himself.

The man said, "I know who you are. Don't let those *cavones* intimidate you. They are all mamas' boys. They wouldn't miss a Sunday seeing their mothers."

They returned to the front room, and Nick poured himself an espresso. The guy who had been on the phone said to the group, "We got a job to do tonight."

While turning to Nick, he asked, "Are you ready to go to work?"

Nick nodded "Yes."

"Good," he said. "Do you know how to drive a truck?"

"Yeah, I can do that," answered Nick.

"Good. You drive tonight, and we'll handle the rest. You just better drive good."

Soon the guy from the back came out and asked them, "Are you guys hungry? I have macaroni for you."

So, the guys ate while they made small talk. Nick listened and took it all in as new names and stories were passed around. He began to feel a little more comfortable.

Later that night, Nick climbed into a truck that was parked on the street in front of the club. He got behind the wheel, while Sal got beside him. Sal directed him through the now quieter streets, into a dimly lit side street, and then into an abandoned area of warehouses. Nick could hear a dog barking in the distance. They sat there for nearly an hour, and suddenly, a trailer truck pulled in with two cars following it.

Sal told Nick, "We gotta move quick now. We gotta get everything loaded fast."

They jumped out and joined the other guys from the club who had come in two separate cars. The driver of the trailer truck pulled open the back doors, and they all started pulling furs off garment racks and piling them in the back of Nick's truck. No words were spoken, and the men moved quickly in the dim light. From the corner of his eye, Nick noticed a big armful of furs being put into the trunk of one guy's car. Nothing was said. Nick climbed back into the truck with Sal. They pulled up to another large warehouse where the two club member cars were already waiting for them. The doors to the warehouse opened, and Nick was told to drive the truck straight in. Their part of the job was done. There were other guys already inside the warehouse that would take over. This time, Nick climbed into the back seat of one of the cars, and they drove straight back to the club.

This was Nick's first real job as a new member of the family, and he felt a great rush of adrenaline. One of the guys broke out the cards. Nick wanted to leave, but something made him stay even though it was getting late. He felt he was getting closer to these men. (Ironically, the feeling of familiarity that comes from knowing the dope and having the goods on someone, is often mistaken as a feeling of closeness. Eventually, familiarity breeds contempt and not closeness at all.) So, Nick read the newspaper and enjoyed a cup of espresso, while listening to the guys talk among themselves. They were figuring out what they would get for the furs, what profit they would make, and what they would have to give to Pope. Nick had the feeling that at least one of the guys resented the boss.

"We have to give that SOB whore, sitting on his ass up there, his take."

Nick realized that the guy complaining was the one who had thrown the furs into the trunk of a car. Nick also knew that his own job was to help Pope get rid of the bad apples, and he knew he would eventually have to turn him in. He thought about how this family was just like any family. If you run to Mommy and tell her your brother ate the cookies, Mommy will call brother in and will ask him, "Did you eat the cookies?" Brother will answer, "No, I didn't eat the cookies." Now whom does Mom believe? Your brother loses trust in you and leaves the room, while you are left with knowing that payback from him is in order in the near future. As a family, no matter what, you're a family. Someone is there that you can always count on. As with most families, however, there is a breakdown in the connection from time to time.

After a while, the guys were finally starting to break up and were saying goodnight. One guy, Frankie, walked over to Nick and invited him over to his house the next day for some food and friendship. Frankie was celebrating his daughter's First Holy Communion. Nick readily agreed to go. "Sure, thanks," he said and went back to his apartment that night feeling good and hoping he was being accepted by at least one of the guys.

Nick went to early Mass the next morning. After Mass, Nick asked one of the sisters from the convent if he could buy a medal of the Virgin Mary as a gift for Frankie's daughter. He then walked to Luigi's Bakery and bought an assortment of Italian pastries. He stopped at a street vendor and bought a dozen roses. A few hours later, he found the address of the duplex that Frankie had given to him. As he walked to the house, he felt a little nervous and had a lump in his throat. This was a feeling he would prefer to lose, and he wondered if it would ever go away. The feeling put him on edge and he just could never become comfortable. Nick rang the doorbell, and the door flew open immediately. He found himself surrounded by at least six or eight screaming little kids. The house seemed to be filled with people, and the noise spilled into the street. He found it a wonder that anyone could even hear the doorbell ring. The girls started screaming for their father to come to the door. Frankie made his way through the crowd and ushered

Nick into the house. He introduced Nick to his wife and mother. Nick gave the roses to Frankie's wife and the box of pastries to his mother, who hurried off with them into the crowd. He then met Frankie's daughter, who had been one of the excited kids at the door, and gave her a box with the medal in it for her First Communion.

Frankie grabbed a glass of wine off a tray passing by and handed it to Nick. Frankie took Nick out back of the house where a few other guys Nick knew were standing around. Some were smoking cigars and telling stories just like any normal guys on their day off. It felt good for Nick to be in this atmosphere. This is what he wanted all along—since he was a teenager—to be a part of a family with its ties and friendships. He felt lucky to have been in the right place at the right time when he met Pope.

CHAPTER 9

Nick did the usual hanging out at the clubs for the next few days. He had found a gym near his apartment and he went every day to work out. For the next few weeks, all was quiet with the family, so Nick spent the remainder of his time doing collections on loans and gambling debts.

The guys told Nick, one day, about a guy from a pawn shop who was not paying up. Apparently, this man had bet on the ponies and owed the family quite a bit of money on a gambling bet. Frankie said it was time they sent over a new face. Frankie and Dominic thought to send Nick as a test to see what he was made of. They would go with him.

They told Nick the story of how this guy had not paid up for months.

"It's gone on for too long," said Dominic. "He's gotta get roughed up. He's gotta pay. This can't get out on the streets that he's not paying; it would not look good."

They drove Nick to the pawn shop, explaining: "This guy needs to be slapped around; he's gotta learn a lesson."

The car pulled to the curb a short distance from the pawn shop.

Nick asked Frankie, "Do you have any old sweatshirts in the back of your car? I wanna wear it, and I need your diamond ring, Frankie."

"What do you need my ring for?"

"Don't worry about it. You'll get it back," answered Nick. As Nick got out of the car, he turned and said to Frankie, "Make sure nobody comes in while I'm in there."

He walked into the pawn shop, and nobody was in there except for behind the counter, where there was a heavyset guy matching the description he had been given by Frankie.

Nick put the diamond ring on the counter and said, "How much could I get for this? What's it worth?"

The guy picked up the ring and the jeweler's glass. As he put the glass to his eye, Nick knew he would be blind on that side and slammed the man's head down on the counter. He then pulled the guy's head back by his hair with his left hand, and whacked him with his forearm to his face. He went down to the floor with force, and Nick jumped over the counter and grabbed him again by the hair.

"Would you like this to continue, or would you like to pay me now? You owe me $1500 on your vig," Nick demanded.

"I'll give it to you! I'll give it to you! It's in the register."

"Don't move," Nick told him, "or I'll finish you off right where you're lying."

Nick took the money from the register, counted it, and picked up Frankie's ring off the counter. "I'll be back every week until your debt is paid off. Leave the money in an envelope on the counter. I don't want to have to go through this again."

He walked out and saw Frankie standing outside.

"Holy shit," said Frankie, "I don't think we'll have any more problems collecting from him again."

Nick asked, "What do you want me to do with this old sweatshirt? I musta busted the guy's nose; there's blood all over the arm. That's what's handy about an old sweatshirt."

Riding back to the club, Nick was still a little shaky. *God, if he had only paid up,* he thought, *I wouldn't have had to do this.*

Back at the club, Nick was asked how everything went.

"Christ," said Frankie, "I can't believe how strong he is!"

Dominic asked Nick that night: "If you go out anytime at night this week, there's a beauty shop on Main Street named Angelo's. I just need a few bullets put into his front windows. He owes for basketball games. I hope he'll get the message. He does all our wives' hair, and they're in love with him. Broken fingers would mean not being able to work, and the last thing we need is a bunch of hysterical wives down our necks."

"No problem," said Nick. "Consider it done."

The weeks flew by, and everybody in the family kept busy doing collections and going about their jobs. Everything seemed calm for a change.

It was a warm sunny morning in April, and Nick woke up that day feeling great with energy and hope. He showered and dressed to go to early Sunday Mass. He nodded to Sal, Dominic, and Frankie before getting into his pew. It seemed as though the whole neighborhood was there.

Then he noticed about 30 children coming up the aisle, accompanied by Sister Mary Joseph, the same sister he had bought the medal from a few weeks back. He then noticed a beautiful young woman walking behind the children, doing her best to keep them in line and moving up the aisle. Sister turned to say good morning to Nick. The young lady looked over and saw Nick.

"Good morning, Sister," he said, while making eye contact with the young woman and smiling at her. She smiled back. The group then took their seats some pews ahead of Nick.

"*Whew,*" Nick said to himself, "*I've got to find out who she is; she is absolutely breathtaking!*"

When he went to Holy Communion, he walked around the pews to take in that lovely face again, but she glanced shyly down as Nick walked past her.

After Mass, Nick noticed that Sister, the children, and the beautiful young woman went down the stairs on the side of the church to the Sunday school rooms in the basement. Nick went up to Frankie, Dominick, and Sal who were standing around doing the usual after Mass chat.

He asked Frankie, "Who's the beautiful young lady with Sister Mary Joseph?"

"Oh boy," said Frankie, "If you know what's good for you, stay away from her!" Nick immediately sensed there was more to that story!

Nick was busy the next few weeks, in and out of towns, taking care of some unfinished business for the family. When he finally got back to the club, Frankie handed him several messages—one of them being a sealed envelope. Nick knew it was from Pope. He put his messages in his coat pocket. He hung around for a while, discussing the business of his trips and handing over a great deal of money he had collected. Afterwards, he read his letter from Pope. Pope expressed his wishes that everything was going well and hoped that Nick felt settled in by now. He reassured Nick that it would not be too much longer until he was back home.

Pope then asked a favor of Nick. "There is a family wedding in a few weeks, and I want you to escort my widowed daughter and granddaughter." He went on to explain that they would be expecting him at 10:30 on that Saturday morning. A car would pick Nick up at 10 o'clock.

The next few weeks flew by. Nick attended the same Mass every Sunday, but didn't see the beautiful young lady again. He could still picture her in his mind

… those big blue eyes and long dark hair. He thought it was better if he didn't see her, but he couldn't get her out of his mind.

The morning of the wedding, Frankie called him and asked if he wanted to come along with the guys. They were heading into the City for a ball game and would be eating in Little Italy afterwards.

"I can't today. I have to take care of a few things. Next time," Nick said.

As he laid out several suits, shirts, and ties, he thought to himself, *"I hate weddings. I'd much rather go to the game with the guys, but there are some things in life you have to do."* After looking through his suits, Nick chose the one he would wear; then the shirt and tie to go with it. He pressed the pants and the front of the shirt. He buffed up the shoes he wanted to wear and sat under his sun lamp to get his color for the day. He then showered, dressed and went outside. The car and driver were there already, waiting to pick him up. They drove for about twenty minutes, and Nick noticed they were in a beautiful neighborhood with large gracious homes. The car pulled up to a gate and the driver spoke through the intercom. The gates swung open, and they drove up to the front of the English Tudor-styled home. Nick went up to the front door and rang the doorbell.

A maid in a crisp, black and white uniform opened the door. "You must be Nick," she said.

"Yes," answered Nick.

"Come in, we've been expecting you," she said as she showed Nick into the living room. Nick looked around the room in awe at the well-appointed furnishings and the artwork. *"Hopefully, someday, I will have reached a point in my life that I can surround myself with all this beauty,"* he dreamed.

He heard the ladies coming into the room and he stood up. He almost fell back into the chair. He was speechless! He could not believe he was in the same room as the beautiful girl from church. *She is Pope's granddaughter!*

The mother introduced herself to Nick at once.

"You must be Nick. I am Mrs. Esposito, but please call me Mary."

Nick shook her hand.

She turned toward her daughter and said, "This is my daughter, Felicia."

He shook Felicia's hand. His face felt like it was on fire; his mouth went dry, and she just smiled up at him.

They gathered their coats and left the house. Michael, the driver, said, "Good Morning, Mrs. Esposito. Good morning, Felicia."

"Good morning, Michael. How's the car?"

"Much better now, since the tune-up. We really should be thinking of getting a new car in the near future."

"You know how my father is, Michael ... He never likes to get rid of things."

They went to the church across town. It was quiet in the car. Nick wanted to say something, but he was still speechless. It was so unlike him to be at a loss for words. Fortunately, Mrs. Esposito broke the silence by asking Nick where he was from, about his Italian origin, and if he came from a big family. Nick explained that he was an only child and came from a small family. He was grateful to be, for once, the one being questioned, and soon found himself easily talking. Mrs. Esposito told him it was great to have her daughter back from a couple of years in Europe, where she had been studying Art History. Mrs. Esposito explained that Felicia's grandfather believed there were many more opportunities beyond what she had been exposed to. He had often told his daughter that he wanted something in life for Felicia.

Nick was sitting in the front of the car with the driver, turning for their conversation. Felicia told Nick about her travels in Europe. She had spent time in Paris, and of course in Italy, attending the finest art schools in the world. The European way had suited her fine—living for the day. She was now in the process of becoming established here in the U.S., with the Metropolitan Museum of Art. She was highly educated and qualified to be a museum curator. So she was looking forward to this next phase in her life, to her adventures in the city, and to eventually settling down.

When they arrived at the church, Nick escorted both of the ladies down the aisle. Mrs. Esposito asked him to enter the pew first, followed by Felicia, and then Mrs. Esposito sat next to the aisle. He was well aware of Felicia sitting next to him, but he allowed enough space between them to be proper.

Somehow, the bride didn't seem anywhere near as beautiful as the girl sitting next to him. The ceremony was lovely, and he fantasized that it was Felicia walking down the aisle towards him. The feelings stirring within Nick, towards Felicia, were making him nervous. *"When I want what I think is love, I will pay for it,"* he thought to himself. *"There will never be any commitments."*

Felicia turned toward him and whispered, "Doesn't the bride look beautiful?"

He nodded his head, realizing he was just her escort for the day.

After the ceremony, they were driven to the country club for the reception. As they walked in, cocktails were being served. Nick stood off to the side as Felicia and her mother were greeted by many family members and friends. Everyone fussed over Felicia, as most had not seen her in a while. Nick walked over to the bar, after pulling his eyes away from her, and ordered a club soda. A few of the younger men struck up a conversation with Nick as he sipped his drink. They seemed to be in their early to mid-twenties, and they chatted easily about sports and current events. A few young ladies soon joined the group, chatting with Nick and including him in their conversations.

After they enjoyed their dinner, one of Felicia's aunts asked, "Why aren't any of you young people up dancing?"

Nick and Felicia laughed and stood up to dance. Nick had wanted to ask her to dance from the beginning, but felt it wasn't his place.

As he held her in his arms for their first dance, he commented, "Everybody is always looking at you."

"I don't think they're looking at me," she laughed, "It's you! They see you with me, but they don't know who you are. You know how fascinated people are by someone who stands out as you do. Thank you for saving my grandfather's life."

Nick felt in heaven for the rest of the evening, sharing Felicia with many who wanted to dance with her. The group of young men Nick had spoken with earlier, seemed to stay away from her when she was around him. He wanted her to join in with them as he kept his distance, and was content watching her enjoy herself. On the way home, Nick tried to figure out a plan to see her again, but her mother did it for him.

"Felicia and I are going into the City next Tuesday. She has a final interview at the museum. Since you have such impeccable taste, Nick, I would love for you to come with us and help us pick out suits and shirts for Grandpa while we're there. His tailor has his measurements, but you could help with picking out the fabric, colors, and all."

Nick responded, "I'd be honored to do that for you and Pope."

"Great. I'll have Michael pick you up at 10:30 on Tuesday morning."

They soon arrived back at their home, and Nick walked them to the door. They both thanked him for being their escort for the wedding. Mrs. Esposito invited him in, but he declined, saying it was a long day and he looked forward to seeing them on Tuesday.

Nick asked Michael to pull over on the way home to make a telephone call. He called the club to see what was going on. There were just a few guys there, so he told them he would stop by in the morning after church. He got back into the car and was dropped off at his apartment. His last thoughts before drifting off to sleep were of John. "*My God,*" he thought, "*maybe John's right. A 9-5 job and the girl of your dreams suddenly doesn't seem so bad.*"

Nick saw Felicia in church the next morning, but they had no time for conversation. The children were all running around and jumping. Nick was afraid to get too close, as they might step on his new shoes, so he stayed back. He just mouthed to her he would see her on Tuesday.

After his stop at the bakery to buy bread and pastries for they guys at the club, Nick was greeted warmly at the club—more for the wonderful bread and pastries he had set down on the table. The old man told them he made some Calzoni for lunch. Nick took a seat and was bull-shitting with the guys, as Frankie and Sonny came in.

Frankie asked Nick how the wedding was, and Nick said, "It was nice. The food was good, and what a sweetheart the mother, Mrs. Esposito is."

"I guess you found out who the young lady is ... and, with blessings from her family yet!" Frankie said.

"They are really nice people," Nick replied with a smile.

They both let it go at that.

The men then discussed what business was coming up next week. There was an airport job involving artwork. Also the usual collections, with people who were not cooperating, that needed to be taken care of in the next few days.

Frankie told them, "The garage needs to be looked into; they're not producing enough cars. We don't know what's going on ... we're just not getting our quota of stolen cars. I thought Tony could look into that, Nick. Check it out for us."

After finishing a few more details about the upcoming business, they were ready to eat. They ate and enjoyed the afternoon with lots of laughs, storytelling, lies, and watching the ball game. By late afternoon, it was time for Nick to go. He went for a long walk on his way home. He looked into storefronts of florists, furniture, and jewelry stores. He wasn't sure what was going on with him. He noticed young lovers strolling arm-in-arm, things he had not paid attention to before. He couldn't wait for Tuesday to come.

CHAPTER 10

The car arrived promptly at 10:30 Tuesday morning to pick him up. Nick awoke early that morning and did his usual routine of shaving, sun lamp, showering, and dressing. He had his clothes laid out from the night before.

He exchanged pleasant words with Michael on the way to the house, mainly about the football game from the Sunday before. Nick rang the doorbell, and Mrs. Esposito opened it; he stepped inside. In a few minutes, Felicia came down the stairs, and he couldn't believe how he felt when he saw her face and her smile again.

Conversation flowed on their way into the City, and soon they dropped Felicia off at the museum for her interview. Nick wished her luck.

"They would be crazy not to hire you," he said as she waved good-bye. They had already made plans to meet for lunch in two hours.

Michael drove on, taking Nick and Mrs. Esposito to see Gino the Tailor. Introductions were made, and Gino brought out fine materials to sort through for Pope's suits. Nick noticed some other materials on another counter across the room and asked what they were. "Oh, you do have good taste," Gino said. "That is my top of the line."

So, from Gino's best fabrics, Nick made the selections for four dark suits, two sports jackets, and six pairs of slacks. Nick had never felt such fine fabrics in his life.

Gino asked Nick if he could take his measurements. "I want to make you a suit; you wearing one of my suits would be the best advertising for me. You'll be pleased."

"You have the highest quality of fabrics and meticulous skill in clothing design," said Nick, thanking him.

Nick needed swatches of fabrics so he could pick out shirts and ties for Pope. Mrs. Esposito was pleased with what Nick had chosen, and they left to go to the restaurant to meet Felicia. She was already there waiting for them when they arrived. She could hardly contain herself; she had been offered the job at the museum! She explained that Saturday night there would be a black tie benefit at the museum.

"And they want me to be there," she explained. "It's an opportunity for me to meet many of their special patrons."

"I hate to do this to you, Nick, but do you have a tuxedo? I would hate to go alone. I mean, would you mind taking me there on Saturday night, if you don't have any plans of course. I know it's short notice, but ..."

Nick smiled, "I would be happy and honored to escort you Saturday night."

After enjoying a wonderful lunch, Nick felt so relieved and comfortable in the company of these two ladies, he could have sat there all afternoon.

He excused himself from the table as the ladies discussed their afternoon plans. He went up to Michael who was waiting by the car, "Do me a favor, Michael? At some point this afternoon, would you go back to the museum and get me literature on all that is in the museum? Here's $50, and this is between you and me."

"I understand, Nick. I hear you," Michael answered.

After lunch, the ladies wanted to be dropped off uptown at the boutiques, so Nick left with Michael for the men's shops where he picked out several shirts and ties for Pope. He also chose four pairs of shoes. He put the items on Pope's account. Then, for himself, he told the couturier he needed a complete new tuxedo, shirts, ties, and new black patent leather shoes. The sleeves and cuffs needed minor alterations and would be ready for him on Friday afternoon. He took Pope's clothing with him.

When he got into the car, Michael showed him what he had picked up for him at the museum. He had pamphlets and literature on the museum's art and exhibits.

Michael and Nick were right on time picking up Mrs. Esposito and Felicia. They were just finishing up, and Felicia was excited about having found a dress that she loved for Saturday night. By then, it was late afternoon, and Nick was dropped off first, as he had business to take care of. He needed to change into his work clothes, as they were going to the airport that evening. As he went into the club, Frankie, Sonny, and a few of the other guys were waiting for him. They hung around and had something to eat, just waiting until 10:00 that night, when a van and two cars would pick them up outside the club and drive them to the airport.

They went straight to a huge, dimly lit warehouse. The security guard was expecting them and opened the gates to pass through.

A whole shipment of oil paintings, art from Europe, was stacked neatly in the center of the vast warehouse, and they started loading up the back of the van with paintings. Nick wondered where the paintings were going. Everything went so smoothly, it was almost too good to be true. They left as quickly as they came. It was hard for Nick to believe how easy it was. Having the right connections was what it was all about. Frankie and Sonny took the van to one of the storage centers owned by The Family. Nick and the others went back to the club. Some of the guys were bitching about the artwork, complaining that art was difficult to get rid of. They didn't think they would get much action from it. Nick sensed an undercurrent of resentment for having to do a job when they didn't know what their cut would be. These were the same guys that threw some furs and suits into their own cars the last time Nick was doing a job with them. After playing cards for a while, Nick called it a night; he wanted to get some rest for handling the business of collections the next day.

CHAPTER 11

Nick awakened early that next morning and got on the road. His first stop was at a pizza shop. He went inside and returned a few minutes later with an envelope. While inside, the guys behind the counter asked how Pope was doing. They seemed to know Pope would be getting out soon. The rest of the day went as he was expecting it to go—no problems with anyone paying up; no hassles. It seemed everyone was happy and making money.

He left the best restaurant for last. He was hugged by the owner, although it was only Nick's second time there. He was treated to a great table. The restaurant was quiet before the dinner crowd came. Mario, the owner, was having a special dish made up for himself and for Nick to eat together.

Before dinner, the owner handed Nick a thick envelope, and Nick put it in the inside pocket of his jacket. The owner went into the kitchen, and the waiter put a fine bottle of Chianti on the table and poured a glass for Nick. Nick could smell great things coming from the kitchen. Several minutes later, a fish dish, a chicken dish, and pasta were brought out, followed by the owner. The owner poured himself a glass of the Chianti and joined Nick for a toast. Dinner was just as delicious as it was the time before when Nick was there. This was the main reason he had saved this place as his last stop in a long day. Nick thanked the owner, and the owner thanked Nick for coming.

Days flew by, Nick was very busy making money, and things were looking good. He picked up his tuxedo on Friday. He tried it on there in the shop and agreed with the tailor that it was a perfect fit.

On Saturday, he went to the florist and had roses sent to the Esposito home. He went running at the track and then worked out at the gym for a while. He relaxed in the afternoon, watching the ballgame and taking a nap.

Felicia called late in the afternoon to thank him for the beautiful roses.

"Mother and I just love the roses," she told him. She said Michael would pick him up at 6:30 that evening. He was glad he had spent a good deal of time studying the books and literature about the museum. Now, if he could only remember who painted what, he would be all right. He knew it was important that, before you do a job, you learn as much as you can on the subject. There were always fewer surprises that way, and it was important to Nick to maintain a sense of control. It was important for him to know all about the museum before he went there.

Michael picked him up promptly at 6:30 and went to Felicia's house. Michael asked him on the way if the literature helped him at all.

"Oh, yeah, it was perfect. It covered more than enough ... and don't forget to keep this between the two of us," Nick said.

The door was opened by Felicia herself. She looked absolutely breathtaking. Nick said, "I have to tell you this. You look gorgeous."

She smiled sweetly at him and told him how handsome he looked. Off to the museum they went.

The museum was decorated beautifully with ice carvings and huge floral bouquets. Nick felt right at home with Felicia by his side. He felt complete, and he knew he had never felt this way before. She took his hand to introduce him to her new boss, the head curator of the museum. When she touched him, a warm feeling went through his body. Nick felt at ease. The information he had learned about the museum had really shown. All were impressed with Nick's ability to chat smoothly about the works of art, and Felicia let him know.

When Felicia went to the ladies room, the women were all asking about him. One lady commented, "I wouldn't let go of him if I were you."

Felicia smiled and thought to herself that she wasn't going to let him get away from her if she had any say in her future plans.

When she came out of the ladies room, Nick was waiting for her. He put out his hand and asked her to dance. Nick wondered if the way she looked at him was the way she looked at all men, or if that look were something special reserved for him.

As they danced, Felicia said, "I didn't know you were so knowledgeable about the arts."

"Before I put myself into any situation," he said, "I need to know what is going on." Turning to her, Nick said, "Everyone is staring at you again, admiring you as usual."

"I told you it's not only me. You are a big hit tonight; you simply impress people wherever you go."

"It's funny how I get stared at only when I'm with you though," he responded.

Well, maybe, it's the two of us," she said.

They were so comfortable with one another all evening. It seemed as if they had been a couple for a long time, instead of being out on only a second date.

Michael was waiting for them when the evening was over. They asked him to take them to Little Italy for some late night desserts and cappuccino. They saw people at the restaurant they knew, and after greetings and dessert, it was almost time for them to say goodnight.

Michael drove to Felicia's house, and Nick walked her to the door.

"Come in for just a minute," she said, as she opened the door. He stepped in and she closed the door gently.

"I want to kiss you goodnight," she said. "You made it so easy for me tonight. I was nervous meeting all the people I will be working with. I guess I will have to bring you to work with me, too, if you can quit your job," she said smiling.

"I've enjoyed being with you, too," he said as he bent over and kissed her. It was a short but warm kiss, and they hugged afterwards. For a split second, Nick thought he would lose himself in her arms.

Felicia thanked him again for a wonderful evening. "Once I get my work schedule, I would love to meet you when you are in the City."

"There is an opera coming soon to the Met, and I would love for you to come with me," Nick said. "I can let you know the details if you are interested."

"I'd love to go," she smiled.

"Okay, I'll call you next Saturday, and we can work it out. I'll see about getting tickets," Nick said.

Nick felt so at peace with himself, he almost fell asleep on the way home with Michael.

CHAPTER 12

Nick knew he had some busy weeks coming up starting on Monday. Frankie had given him the details, and Nick realized he would be on his own in his first big job.

The family owned an old, rundown auto mechanic and body repair garage that was abandoned and decaying. It was to be Nick's job to totally renovate the building and clean up the property. Their goal was to have an up and running, fully legitimate garage where mechanical and auto body repairs would be done. The back would be set up as a chop shop where stolen cars and parts would be dismantled, painted and sold.

Nick had already spent time going over paperwork. He had done his research as to how this type of business operated. He made the rounds of the foreign import car dealers—from Ferrari to Jaguar—the body shops, mechanics shops for parts, and also learned the painting process.

He found the old building to be not much more than an existing shell of a structure. Nick worked with all the local tradesmen in order to ensure silence as to what would really be going on inside the building. He also studied government regulations to be sure everything would be in order to the outside world. The place needed a total overhauling—plumbers, painters, carpenters, and sign makers. He learned prices of equipment and new lifts. He studied government regulations. He wanted to make sure everything would be in order to the outside world. The place needed a total overhauling.

Nick had walls knocked down. False floors were installed for the legitimate part of the business, and the stolen car chop shops were underground. Nick had no problems with the layout of what he wanted done. Once things were in motion, Nick oversaw the process clearly and effortlessly. He was successfully managing to transform this filthy, dirty, dingy building into a beautiful state-of-the-art garage. Nick was quite excited about actually seeing the completion of this project from start to finish. He knew he would turn it around in three to four months. Nick saw a need in the area for a specialty garage for foreign import cars in both the front and the back. Soundproof false flooring would separate upstairs from the chop shop below.

Nick even consulted Felicia about the interior of the reception area. He wanted a woman's touch for the interior design. It was important to Nick that women would be comfortable in what is really a man's world of automobile service. Foreign cars were just beginning to become more popular in the U.S., so Nick thought the timing would be just right to go in the direction of a foreign automobile garage. Word reached Nick that Pope thought he was doing a great job. As a matter of fact, Frankie and all the boys were very impressed by Nick's progress.

Frankie knew a number of mechanics and Nick interviewed them, did the hiring and set up the rules. They were to be clean-shaved, with short haircuts and were to wear the uniform Nick had designed with Felicia's input. Each man was given three uniforms and a cleaning service for them. He told each of them: "No drinking on the job, and no slobs will work here." He taught them all how to greet and treat customers. They were to be trustworthy, honest, and reliable. "We will be a respected, legitimate business," Nick said. A special crew of mechanics and painters were brought in for the stolen car section downstairs. They would repaint and resell the cars to car lots, or chop them up for parts to sell.

The work ran just a little over the schedule for completion. Some brickwork remained to be done, but that didn't matter to Nick. He knew Pope was getting out soon, and he wanted Pope to attend his Grand Opening ceremony—complete with caterers and a classic car showing.

Felicia enjoyed her part in choosing the office and waiting room furniture, and Nick enjoyed their time together. For hours they would look over catalogs and visit showrooms.

They met with students studying graphic design at the local college, to assist them in theme design and with putting the final touches on the place. Logos of the cars they would service were painted on the walls. In addition, vintage and classic car prints hung in the waiting room. Nick loved the lines and curves of the graphics—realistic yet abstract enough to hold the viewer's interest. Patriotic colors were used in décor for the auto manufacturing countries of Italy, Germany,

England, and Sweden. Everything blended in beautifully, and Nick was so pleased. The entire project was perfect—from the awnings right down to the rest rooms. It was quite the talk of the area, and Nick's competitors came to check it out.

Pope sent a message to Nick through his daughter, Mary, requesting that Nick drive alone to the prison for his release. The rest of the family thought Pope was getting out two days later than he actually was. Pope wanted a few days of quiet time before seeing anyone.

So, Nick drove to the prison and waited outside for Pope to be released. Nick and Pope embraced as Pope stepped out of the prison gates, a free man again. Pope looked good. He was wearing an older suit and shoes, and looked a bit pale, but he seemed in good physical shape. He told Nick he felt great.

Once in the car, Pope directed Nick to a small Italian restaurant where no one would know them. Pope had been looking forward to his first meal of real food for a long time. They both enjoyed the meal and had a long conversation. Nick confirmed what Pope already knew about what had been happening in The Family. Pope just listened, and at the end of the meal, had many questions for Nick.

They were soon back in the car and on their way to Pope's home where his daughter and granddaughter were anxiously waiting for him.

They were greeted by Felicia, running past the housekeeper to give her grandfather a big hug and kiss. They were so delighted to see each other; it had been such a long time since they had seen one another, as Felicia had been in Europe prior to Pope being sent to prison. Nick went into the kitchen for a glass of water while the family continued their greetings.

Pope just wanted to take a long, hot shower and to put on his pajamas and bathrobe. He left them for a while. When he came back downstairs, he invited Nick to stay, but Nick declined saying he had some things to check out. Nick wanted Pope and his family to have some alone time and catch up on family matters.

Later in the evening, Pope had a discussion with Felicia about Nick and their relationship. He could see by the way Felicia's eyes lit up every time Nick's name was mentioned that everything was fine between them. She told her grandfather how hard Nick had been working on the garage. "You won't believe how beautiful it is; it really is a work of art." She also told him how she helped Nick, giving him her female perspective. "He is so excited you gave him the opportunity and he can't wait for you to see it."

Opening Day of the garage was finally here—a beautiful Sunday afternoon. Invitations had been sent out from mailing lists that Nick organized of owners of foreign cars. The local television, radio stations, and news reporters were all invited.

The classic cars that Nick had brought in were placed in the body shop and out in the front. The mechanics and car painters were all on hand to answer any questions. The two women hired for the front office were busy making appointments for those wanting to bring their cars in for the following weeks.

At one point during the party, Nick overheard two competitors begin to mouth off to each other in raised voices. He went over to them and put his hand on the shoulder of the bigger guy. Very quietly he said, "Not here." Both men walked away from each other and headed in opposite directions. All walks of life came together that day under one roof.

The caterers did a fine job of passing around tray after tray of elegant hors d'oeuvres. The flowers were exquisite, and the whole day was a success. It impressed everyone, especially Pope. The press took pictures and interviewed Nick.

Pope pulled Nick aside and could hardly express how impressed he was.

"I guess I gotta get used to this hi-tech world that is passing me by. I can see how you have to spend money to make money. When I was told some of the costs involved, I had my doubts, but now I see it is money well spent."

Nick responded by telling Pope, "I think we should do another one—maybe 50 or 60 miles from here, in an affluent suburb such as this one."

Pope smiled, "I have another one of my businesses that I need for you to bring up to standard. I need some of our own businesses fixed first, and then we can talk about opening a new one in a year or so."

Everyone went home happy and content. The afternoon had been such a great success. The very next day, they were officially open for business.

CHAPTER 13

My life soon settled into a routine—as much as life could be settled—in the middle of a foreign jungle. As soldiers in Vietnam, we knew what we had to do every day. Yet, every day was different than the other ones. We never knew what to expect when we did our daily patrols, stopping trucks, going through villages looking for supplies and the enemy. Anybody could be the enemy—man, woman, or child. We would seize any weapons we could, even off of dead bodies. We sometimes left the villages burning to the ground as we moved on to our next mission.

The traps and mines were the worst. They killed and maimed more Americans than actual gunfire. We learned to look for the signs, but even then, there were many casualties from them. We knew there would be some mines every day, but we never knew when our meals would be interrupted by simple gunfire. So, the routine was never dull and the men and I realized we could never really sleep, never really relax and could never be caught off guard anytime, anywhere.

What I looked forward to the most was mail from home. Letters exchanged between Elizabeth and me were always filled with hope and promises of things to come.

My letters to my parents always reassured them of my safety and well being. I needed to protect all of them from what the reality of this war was. They only knew what they read in the newspapers of the daily body count coming from Vietnam. There was no need to worry them about what I was facing every day and night.

My family loved sending packages from home, especially my grandmother who sent some of the best baked pastries the guys had ever had—even if they were a bit stale and broken when they arrived. All of the men shared the contents of their packages, so there was usually something to be passed around whenever the supply truck caught up with us.

My grandmother would also send me dry salami, provolone, and pepperoni packed in tins for freshness. But, by the time they were opened, the smell was so strong and bad that everybody would back away. I would cut off the dried sections with my trusted knife and pass it around. Malcolm was the only one that would never taste it. The guys teased me, saying this was all they needed to kill the enemy.

There was never time to really think about anything in depth, but once in a while, I would think about Nick and what different, yet similar, lives we were both leading.

I knew that in Nick's world, you didn't trust anyone either; they could turn on you in an instant. Nick trusted only his own instincts, as he could never be sure of who his enemy was. My world was very similar to Nick's, and I realized we were both leading parallel lives—with only one major difference. For me, the government was The Boss. With Nick, the head guy was The Don; i.e., "The Godfather." While our government could sanction killings for the sake of peace, it was The Don who could okay killing to keep the peace.

I also thought of the dissimilarities between Nick and myself. As much as the overall picture might appear the same, I was living or surviving in the hot sweaty jungles of Vietnam; Nick was living in clean, comfortable surroundings. I would be so grateful to receive simply dry, clean socks from Supply. Nick's clothing, by anyone's standard, was expensive and in good taste.

A relatively quiet time was soon disturbed by the capturing of one of the soldiers in my platoon. The guy had just stepped a few yards away for a smoke, and he was gone. The rest of us couldn't sleep at night, thinking of plans to recapture him. It took almost five days, but we found the village where our buddy was being held captive. There were several Americans being held prisoners in small bamboo cages—too small to stand up in. Each cage had a guard 24 hours a day. So, my men and I knew we had to kill all the guards at precisely the same time, or the Americans would be shot. We planned for the attack to take place in the middle of the night, and it was executed without error. We rescued our American soldiers. Their fingers had been broken, and they had been tortured with bamboo splints pushed up under their fingernails. Hatred for the enemy was stronger now that our men had personally encountered such brutality. We became more confident in our marksmanship and in our courage.

It wasn't long after we had settled into camp in the early evening, that we could hear the mortars and artillery starting. Malcolm and I ran out of camp a few hundred yards to find cover. We soon realized we couldn't just stay there, so we circled from behind where the mortars were coming from, and saw a group of six or eight enemy soldiers shooting at our camp. Malcolm and I opened fire and wiped every one of them out.

Then, there was the night that began as any other ordinary night. It was hot, and we were tired as we set up camp. We had been walking all day through the crude trails and we just wanted to kick back and relax for a few hours before taking turns at guard duty.

We cleaned up after chow when we heard artillery starting. We knew right away that it was close and that it was meant for us.

Mortars and shelling began coming in from over a ridge that was above us. The dark night sky was exploding around us. Men were scattering everywhere. Explosions were going on, and there was smoke everywhere. The GI's were yelling obscenities and screams were heard.

"I'm not gonna die here!"

"What the fuck are we doing?"

Malcolm grabbed me and said, "Let's get the fuck out of here."

We knew we couldn't just stay there and shoot back at a faceless enemy in the dark. Our instincts and our training told us there were probably six or eight Vietnamese firing at us.

I yelled to Malcolm: "We gotta stop them! We gotta get up and around them."

Malcolm yelled back, "Follow me!"

Flashes of light blinded us as we half-ran, half-crawled up the hill. We felt like screaming and yelling. The energy, the excitement was almost overwhelming. We felt as if our legs were not even under us and as if we were going to burst into an explosion. That is exactly what it took for us to kill.

Reaching the top of the edge, we hit the ground on our bellies, gasping for air.

I looked at Malcolm and said, "Let's do it."

We crawled through the brush to come in behind the enemy. We threw our grenades and opened fire; there was no such thing as overkill.

Malcolm was just ahead of me when I saw the flash. I knew Malcolm took a bullet in the leg, but Malcolm never flinched; he just kept right on shooting.

After what seemed like forever, there was silence. On my belly, I made my way up to Malcolm.

"Don't you dare fucking leave me here," he said.

I used my shirt to put pressure on the wound and told Malcolm it was only a flesh wound, and Malcolm was up in no time. We crawled down over the ridge and counted six bodies of the enemy. We kicked the bodies over and put a few more shots into them just to be sure.

We yelled down to our men, "We're up here! It's us!"

Dead silence met us again in the night.

Malcolm said, "I'll yell down; no mother fucking Cong can mimic *my* accent."

A voice from below yelled, "I'd recognize that voice anywhere; it's Malcolm. Nobody else can say 'motherfucker' quite like that!"

I helped Malcolm down the hill and joined up with our men. As they came closer, Malcolm and I realized that three of our own men were killed in the ambush, and two were wounded.

Getting back to what was left of our camp, we cleaned the wounds. Malcolm was still wincing with pain as he said, "No way am I reporting this wound. I don't wanna be taken away now. After all," he smiled, "what would you do without me, Johnny?"

We radioed for a helicopter to come and pick up the bodies of our comrades and the wounded. Replacements for them would be arriving almost immediately.

With seven months of our tour of duty almost over, John and Malcolm and the other experienced soldiers now knew what it was like to be given rookies into their platoon. They knew that if it hadn't been for the experience they had under their belts, that they would have been dead by that last attack. No amount of instinct or courage could replace just living, breathing, and sleeping in that hell for almost a year of your life.

When things settled down once more, I worried that I was becoming such a different man than the boy I had been when I volunteered my life for the sake of my country. I felt so changed that I wondered if I could even have a normal relationship with Elizabeth when I returned home. I could sleep only three or four hours a night. I would wake startled and jump up ready to fire. I didn't realize it was going to be normal to want to kill for survival. I knew I wasn't alone in my thinking; I could see it in the cold stone eyes of the men. They said nothing about their fears and kept them hidden inside themselves.

It was like taking a hard blow to the gut to realize that this was not a war about freedom at all. This was a political war and a good number of soldiers were making a fortune in the Black Market, hoarding the cash to take home with them.

They were making their time worthwhile, feeling what they were doing was not dishonest or corrupt, but rather the government owed them for taking their freedom as civilians away for a year or so. Dealings in alcohol, drugs, cigarettes and food were common, and everybody turned their heads to it. I realized that Nick was not wrong about power, money, and greed. What a waste of time and life this was!

After the attack, we were called back in to regroup for a couple of days. Malcolm's wound was cleaned. "Just a scratch," said the doctor after giving him a shot of penicillin for infection. Hot showers were a bonus; they felt like heaven for those few too brief moments.

The men saw the new rookies arriving with sparkles in their eyes.

"God, were we ever that green?" Malcolm asked me. "They look like young choirboys. I wonder what we look like to them. Boy, a year here makes a big difference. Can you imagine what they'll look like in six months?"

"Yeah," I said, "if they make it!"

After a few more days of hanging around, waiting for new recruits to arrive, an explosion was heard coming from the barracks. It was late in the afternoon, and a whole shipment of rookies were waiting around to see what would happen next. Suddenly, men were running everywhere; it was chaos for awhile. Some soldiers grabbed a young Vietcong boy as he was running from the barrack area. Others had actually seen him throw the grenade and had shouted, but it was already too late.

A soldier yelled, "Go get Jumpin' Joe; this kid is going for a ride."

Within a matter of minutes, a helicopter landed. Two of the guys pulled the kid into the helicopter and the helicopter took off. One of the new recruits standing near me asked, "What is that all about?"

I said, "Don't worry; they're just going to give him a ride home. He'll be dropped off at his village … if you know what I mean."

I turned to the rookie again and said, "The sorry part is that it doesn't stop. There will be another one tomorrow—a young boy, an old man, or a pregnant woman."

I told the rookie, "Let me give you a little piece of advice: don't stand in line for food; always wait till the end of the line. Don't expose yourself, and don't ever stand still for too long—anywhere."

Word was going around that some Brass were coming in to give medals and awards to those who were still alive. I was one of those who got a message to report to the Captain's quarters. Once inside, the Brass proceeded to commend me for my bravery, skill, common sense, and my mutual feeling for soldiering. They presented Malcolm and me with a Medal of Commendation.

CHAPTER 14

It was the beginning of a typical, unbearably hot day as I stepped outside into the Vietnam sunlight. I took a few steps and stopped to reflect on where I was, where I had been and where I was going. In my letter to Nick, only the night before, I had written:

The longer I stay here, the more of what you said is coming true. The streets of the U.S. are the same. There are even rumors that the U.S. Government is involved here with dealing drugs, women, and bribery; that the corruption goes right to the top. Some of these people are making a lot of money. I'm beginning to see that you and I are really not that different. I wear a U.S. Government-issued uniform, so that is supposed to make what I am doing all right. Keep in touch. Hope all is well with you. Looking forward to talking to you in person. John

My typical morning was suddenly jolted into frenzy right after Malcolm and I stepped into the breakfast chow line. A shot was heard and somebody went down in the line. Everyone scattered. We all ducked for cover, and I asked Malcolm what direction the shot had come from. Malcolm said, "Around 11 o'clock." The lieutenant and the major both came out looking for me.

The major handed me a rifle and said, "Try this weapon, but be careful because you might fall in love with her."

Malcolm was then asked by the major if he knew where the shot came from.

"Yes, sir, I do," he said.

Malcolm and I left from the side of the building and went to a location where we could get a clearer shot. I was carrying the major's custom-made sniper rifle, unlike any weapon I had ever seen.

Malcolm said, "Don't look for a person because he'll be covered with leaves and stuff. Look for the rifle." He suddenly stopped and pointed. I raised the rifle and looked through the telescope toward the trees and within a few minutes, the sniper was located. I now had a bead on the guy's head.

"I'm glad you told me to look for the guy's rifle," I whispered to Malcolm, and then pulled the trigger. A loud crack sounded and, in moments, I heard a body falling through the trees to the ground. Malcolm and I walked back to the Captain's headquarters, where he and the Major were out front. The Major asked me how I liked the rifle and I laughed, saying: "I'm in love."

The Major said, "I'm changing my location for now, so I'm gonna leave the rifle with you, John. I had someone else in mind to complete a mission for me, but now I know I want you to do the job. I will get you the coordinates, pictures, and location by tomorrow. This is a big job, and it will require a lot of patience and steady nerves, both of which I know you have. It should take several days for you, Malcolm, plus three other guys, to complete the mission. Be here by ten tomorrow morning and we'll go over the details."

The events of this day pumped up our adrenaline. By nightfall, Malcolm and I were both excited.

"I like having a specific job to accomplish," I said to Malcolm. "I like plans and deadlines and orderly lines rather than chaos. Our special assignment from the major will be an interesting challenge."

At 7 a.m. the next day, we reported to the Captain. He sat us down and began to explain in detail what the mission was all about. He went over the map with us, indicating the best routes to take, using truck transportation to a certain location, and then showed where we would walk to our place to stay away from our hit. At a precise location we would be airlifted out.

"The hit," he explained, "is targeted for an organizer and high ranking leader in the Vietnam army. Right now, according to our intelligence, he is at this base. He is in the process of organizing a massive group of men, and he needs to be stopped. He's in charge and very capable. Removing him will create a month or two more of chaos and confusion for them, perhaps stopping the buildup altogether."

Maps of the terrain were given, showing areas of jungle concentration that Malcolm and I were used to by now.

"You should be able to take him down within half a mile or more with the telescope on the rifle, I gave you," the major said.

That evening at dusk, Malcolm and I gathered the supplies and equipment we would need to survive in the jungle for a week or so. The truck transported us to a point three or four miles north of our assigned location. We were quiet the first hour or so in the truck, talking mostly about the shelter and protection we would need upon arrival at our destination. We agreed to stay about a mile off of our directed course on the map. We had learned to never do exactly what everyone else expected, including the enemy.

We were almost at our destination, and I began putting on my face camouflage. When I handed Malcolm some black face paint, he laughed.

"You're not seeing my color, are you, Johnny?"

Malcolm is the only one who called me "Johnny" except for Nick, and that personal familiarity helped me to feel more at home and comfortable.

I told him, "I was brought up that the test of a man isn't based on his color, but on what he's worth. My folks had to struggle too." Some people likened us to each other. Malcolm and I hit it off after that day and had great respect for each other.

It was pure black at night when we were dropped off. It was a perfect night for us: rainy and dark. We hiked to our location with Malcolm leading the way. I was in the middle of the group, protected on both sides. Malcolm found the spot to spend the next few hours setting up protection from the weather. We had four hours until sunrise and took turns on guard.

We were all up at sunrise, and since we were on a ridge, we could survey the land below and figure out the best route to take without being seen or heard. We dried our wet clothes in the early morning sun. We had some chow, but no fires.

All was quiet and so unusual from what we were so used to. We arrived late afternoon at the highest point possible for setting up camp. We climbed up three hills to where we felt we could protect ourselves best.

We laid back and rested. We wanted a good night's sleep. We wanted to be up before sunrise the next day for approaching the target area and getting a closer look at what was going on. We awoke two hours before sunrise and Malcolm and I left quietly to scout out the area. The other guys stayed behind to keep the camp secure for our return, using natural camouflage and digging in.

Malcolm and I reached a high point within a half mile of our target. With binoculars, we saw the base and several areas of rising smoke with about 2-3,000 men all in training programs. We moved around the circumference of the base to find the right location for hitting my target. We stayed until dusk, getting closer and closer. We observed our target and watched him all day so we would know his every move. All seemed clear in all directions. We repeated the procedure for the next two days, observing our target's exact movements from sun up to sun down. He was regimented and we were able to memorize his schedule. We decided to go after our target when the Viet Cong were receiving training for their rifles. In the midst of their firing exercises, no one would ever hear the crack when I pulled my trigger.

On the last day of observing, we went over every maneuver again. We knew we were as ready as we were ever going to be. Since I was shooting from such a long distance, only weather and wind would affect the timing of the mission.

We were up before sunrise the next morning. Malcolm and I approached our designated location according to schedule. The camp was very much alive with training programs in progress, heavy-duty equipment and men moving into camp. The Viet Cong were building up quite an offense.

We spotted our specific Viet Cong target. Malcolm whispered to me how incredible it was that we were going to take this guy out from this distance, and the guy would never know what hit him. I kept a bead on our target after I spotted him. Watching the enemy from a distance didn't seem like the jungle warfare we had experienced close-up and face-to-face. I couldn't get over the fact that the guy would die when I decided it was time. It was an incredible feeling of power.

The target was now 30 yards within their rifle range. I wanted to wait until he approached the line of shooters, and waited for the rapid firing of several guns in the line. With that, our target went down, Malcolm turned, and I followed, and we ran and ran for two and a half miles to meet up with the other guys.

We came upon our own men with no noise coming from behind us. The confusion we left behind us, made it that much easier for all of us to be in the clear. Malcolm was in front of me and yelled to the guys: "Get the mother-fucking helicopter! Get us the hell out of here!" Just as he spoke the words, a helicopter came out of nowhere to pick us up. We ran to the clearing and were whisked away into the Vietnamese sky. We congratulated ourselves on a new accomplishment for the Unit. I had an adrenaline rush but remained quiet. I was tired and mentally drained. I looked forward to a meal and rest after reporting to my Captain.

As soon as we landed in a clearing at camp, I left the group to find the captain. I found him in his headquarters. I saluted the captain and told him, "Mission accomplished without incident. It was quite an incredible experience."

The Captain said, "I'll have another mission for you within the week. The upper brass will be happy, as they wanted to have the marines become more involved in sniper shootings. You and a chosen few will be the new extension of what the marines can accomplish. Because of men like you, we will be able to develop this new asset of the marines. You and your men will have leave for the next few days. You look like hell now. Go get yourself a good meal, shower, and some sleep. As soon as I hear from the upper brass, I will call for you and let you know what they have to say."

I left the Captain's quarters. The men were gathering around, as word had quickly spread about the incredible mission we had just accomplished. I talked briefly with the men and soon left them to get myself a shower and a hot meal. I was too wound up and too overtired to actually relax and get sleep. I thought of Elizabeth and began writing a letter.

The captain sent for me the next day. He had spoken to the upper brass, and it was determined that we had handled our mission perfectly. They knew from their intelligence that the Viet Cong camp had no idea where the shot at them had come from. Break-up of their camp followed the chaos. Since they knew they had been discovered, their men were being dispersed. They feared a heavy artillery or air attack from us. So, our mission was a complete success all around. The captain told me we would be getting orders in the next day or two for the next kill.

In the meantime, the Captain took me aside and told me, "We've been following your progress, going by the records of your marksmanship as a rookie. There are very few with your abilities. Your calmness and your keeping a cool head makes you a perfect candidate for what we would like you to become. When your tour of duty is over here, we would like you to stay on with the U.S. Government as a member of a very small, elite group of men. Your excellent marksmanship would be essential to your job. I can't give you any more information at this time. I don't need an answer today or tomorrow. I want to give you time to think about it. I do not want you to mention this conversation to anyone else. I understand you and Malcolm are one hell of a team, but do you trust him with your life?"

I did not hesitate for an instant before answering, "Absolutely, Sir. Without a doubt, Sir!"

"Okay, so think about what I've said, and when I return in a month or so, we will talk more. It could mean a secure future for you; working for the government has its benefits."

The first thing I thought as I left the Captain was: *"Holy Shit! They want me to be a hit man. I can't wait to tell Nick this one!"*

I just hung out, waiting for my next orders. I was still excited about the mission, but couldn't understand why I liked what I did. I thought about my future as a sniper assassin and felt I might be stuck in this job that the government wanted me to do, even after Vietnam. I thought about the results and the consequences of what I would be doing. If it helped the security of my government and the safety of the people's lives, then I knew this type of work had to be done. I thought about having this as a secret part of my life. Could I live a normal life and keep this deep secret from Elizabeth in the civilian world?

One mission led to another, and for the next couple of months, Malcolm and I were rarely seen apart. I realized how important Malcolm was to me. We had many discussions about our future and how we both felt about doing this in the real world. We both agreed that the results we saw far outweighed the negative affects of this job, and it was necessary to continue this life after the Marines. We were convinced that the people we eliminated were a threat to so many lives, and that the world was a better place without them.

We were told that once we arrived back in the States, we would be called in to receive more info and training in the civilian world. Our new job would be different from the one in the jungles of Vietnam. Before we knew it, our tour had come to an end, and we were preparing to go home—alive and in one piece.

Our feelings about leaving were not what we expected. It was a somber time for us. We finally arrived in Saigon, on buses similar to those we had come in on a year ago. My mental state was the same as a year ago also: not knowing what to expect, coupled with a lot of mixed feelings. I hoped that once I got home, things would go back to normal, whatever "normal" was. I realized everyone was silent on the bus. I guessed everybody felt something was going to go wrong. We were brought to the plane on the tarmac, and everyone boarded in silence.

"Just get this plane off the ground and get the hell out of here!" someone shouted. The plane turned, and as it began its ascent, wheels lifting off the ground, the cheering started. Someone yelled, "Good-bye suckers, I'm going home!" The plane climbed, and the pilot came on. Seatbelt signs were off. Everybody was up, and it was like New Year's Eve. We talked about things we hadn't talked about in a year: our girlfriends, our wives, our families, our future plans and education. But, I knew there was an underlying fear about returning to the civilian world again and fitting into a society that had unknown changes awaiting us. Were we going to be ready for that?

CHAPTER 15

We flew to Hawaii, refueled, had a few hours to stretch our legs, and realized we were back in the United States when we saw the largest American flag we had ever seen. Upon our arrival at Camp Pendleton in California, we went through our debriefing and were soon being discharged from the Marine Corps. We went to the PX to buy our clothes for returning home to civilian life.

I said to Malcolm, "The only good part of this for us, Malcolm, is that we'll still be working together, and the rest of these people we'll probably never see again."

We hugged and said, "I'll be seeing you."

With that, I waited for the plane to New York to take me home. I had talked to my family on the phone, so they were anxiously expecting me. My mother and Elizabeth met me at the airport. I hugged them both at once and nobody wanted to let go. It seemed as if we were embraced for hours.

When we finally pulled apart, I asked, "Where's Dad?"

"Dad's home cooking; waiting for you with his emotions. If he's going to cry, he wants to cry in his own yard."

When we got home, the yard was filled with family, friends, and neighbors. My dad had been cooking up a storm: wild mushrooms, sausage and peppers and the homemade wine was being brought up from the cellar. I saw my Dad and embraced him. He quickly left the room to hide his emotions. I held my grandparents close to me. Everyone was hugging and crying. I tasted the food I had only dreamed of for a year; it was even better now than I remembered. I never let go of Elizabeth's hand all night.

I looked around for Nick and asked Elizabeth if he was coming. She said, "He will be coming tomorrow when you two will have more time to talk."

The evening came to an end with all the good-byes.

Elizabeth and I stayed up late, holding each other and talking. I began to feel a bit jumpy as the night wore on, listening to the sounds of the neighborhood. My hearing had become so acute that my ears were sensitive to sound. Elizabeth finally had to leave, as she had school the next day, followed by her job in a small card shop.

I realized I would not be able to sleep in my bedroom that night, so I took a blanket from the house and found myself looking for a protected area in the yard and an advantage point. I chuckled to myself over what I was doing. I got my usual three-and-a-half to four hours of sleep, awakening at sunrise, feeling startled, not knowing where I was. I grabbed for my rifle that wasn't there, realizing I would need to adjust to my new life. I went into the house to make coffee, and my grandfather came down to the kitchen.

He said, "You haven't slept in the yard since you were a child. You always loved it."

We sat together outside, having our coffee.

Grandfather said, "Nick's a good boy and a good friend. While you've been away, he's been in touch with Elizabeth and us, always asking if we needed anything. Good friends are hard to come by. I'm going to go to the garden now to do some weeding and watering."

"I'll be out to help you if you need it," I said. I went and got my knife and walked behind the garage where the vegetable gardens were. My old target was still on the garage wall. I threw the knife, and it landed right in the middle.

My grandfather looked up and said, "I've never seen you throw from the hip before—let me see you do that again."

Then, he said, "Here! John!"

Startled, I turned to find my grandfather throwing me a pitchfork, saying "Help me with this pile." I grabbed the pitchfork with my left hand and held it like a rifle and went down on one knee. That was my first flashback.

He was surprised at how I reacted and he said, "You don't realize it yet, but you need your time to adjust."

I laughed and said, "I am already beginning to realize that."

"What are your plans for today, John?" he asked.

I was expecting to see Nick in the morning, but I didn't mention it. Elizabeth called to say hello before she left for school. She wanted to tell me she missed me and loved me and couldn't wait to see me at dinnertime that night.

Meanwhile, my grandmother and my mother were very emotional. Every time they came near me, they hugged me and cried. I showered and had my favorite breakfast. I couldn't finish it; I wasn't used to eating this much anymore.

As I was leaving the house for a walk through my neighborhood, I said, "Tell Nick, if he comes, I'll be at the beach—near the ball field."

As I approached the ball field, I heard the sounds of kids playing. Soccer practice was going on; it was the Catholic Grammar School team that was on the field. The coach was a friend of mine, a guy with whom I had played soccer while in grade school. We hugged each other. He told me: "Watch these guys and feel free to help me out here."

I felt for the moment, that I had never left. It was good to hear children playing and having fun. There were no worries of the world on the playing field. I did give some advice to the kids, showing them maneuvers in kicking and controlling the ball.

I looked up and saw a strong image by the side—a well-dressed and tanned man. I knew immediately who it was; Nick would stand out anywhere. I ran over and we embraced. We walked to the beach and talked for hours, bringing each other up to date. Nick talked about his business startups and about meeting the love of his life, Felicia.

"I can't wait for you to meet her—you and Elizabeth come into the city, and the four of us will get together and spend time. A friend of mind has a beautiful boat, and I made arrangements for you and Elizabeth to go on it any time."

I said, "Elizabeth will have to come up with an excuse for her parents to be able to spend a night on the boat."

Nick said, "Just give me a call ahead of time."

I said, "Thanks. That will be terrific."

Of course politics were brought up and I told Nick about the government's offer of joining them and becoming a sharpshooter.

Nick responded, "So they want you to become a legal hit man. I still think you should come with us and make some real money for doing the same thing. If you go with the government, it'll be like we're partners doing some projects together."

"Nick, you know how I feel about your way of life. I respect you, but I feel it's a one way situation—you'll come out of it either dead or in jail."

Nick responded, "What the hell do you think your job is? Someday you'll realize it's all the same. Any time you need some confidential street info about anywhere in the world, I can help you."

I said, "And I'm telling you that if there were anything that you need to hear, I would let you know."

Nick said, "I told you we were partners."

I smiled and said, "Best friends is more like it."

"Come on, let's go for a hot dog," said Nick. So we went to our favorite stand, ran into some old friends, and we all tried to catch up.

Nick said, "I want to come see your parents, but let's stop at the bakery and the fruit store to buy peaches for making Papa's wine. I always loved your grandfather's wine after the peaches have soaked in it for a day or so."

We went to the house and had a great time with homemade wine and cheese. Grandmother had just made loaves of hard crusted bread. We spent the afternoon talking about the war and how everyone coped while I was away.

Elizabeth came over between her classes and work. Nick and Elizabeth were so glad to see each other.

"I don't know how I would have gotten through it without your confidence that John was coming home," she said to Nick. "And thank Felicia for calling; we have a friendship now."

"Yeah," Nick said, "Felicia is looking forward to actually meeting you. I was just telling John how I want you to come into the city so the four of us can go out together."

We promised we would stay in close touch with each other as Nick was leaving to go back to the city. Nick gave me his private number, saying: "Call me day or night. Elizabeth already has it, but now I'm giving it to you."

CHAPTER 16

The next few weeks, I was still having a hard time adjusting. I talked to Malcolm in Detroit, and I always felt better after talking to him. Malcolm was going through similar feelings, so it made me feel better that it was normal for him to not want to be in crowded areas where people were moving in different directions. He would survey an area before approaching and would be easily startled by loud noises, quick movement, or even the wind in the trees and the leaves rustling across the yards.

I was looking forward to spending some time alone with Elizabeth—more than a few hours a night. Elizabeth told her parents a fictional story for us to be able to spend our first entire weekend together. Nick made all the arrangements for us to have use of his friend's boat.

Elizabeth and I were shocked to see the size of the boat. It was a sixty-five-foot yacht. The guard walked us down the dock to the boat and handed me the keys. "If you need anything, let me know," he said.

We let ourselves onto the boat and Elizabeth said, "I have never seen anything like this in my life! Whose boat do you think it is?"

I said, laughing, "You probably don't want to know."

On the table, there was a beautiful bouquet of flowers and a bottle of champagne with a note. The note said: "Enjoy!"

We explored the boat and were amazed at the furnishings, the paintings, upper decks, lower decks, and the equipment on board.

"We could just live here," said Elizabeth.

I said, "I don't want this weekend to ever end."

We took the champagne and two glasses to the upper deck outside and we toasted to each other and to our future.

As we sat there gazing at the sky and the stars, I became rather quiet. All was still and Elizabeth asked me what was wrong.

I replied, "I'm so used to looking at the sky at night to determine our fate. A still night like this one is rare. Usually, in Nam, night was filled with tracers, smoke, and explosions."

With that, Elizabeth got up to embrace me, becoming one. She took my hand and said, "Maybe it's time to go below now." And we did.

The weekend was a separation from all life as we knew it. I wondered why life couldn't just always be like this.

I called Nick the following day, on the private number he had given to me. While on the phone, we made plans for the four of us to get together in the city on that following Saturday. Both Felicia and Elizabeth were anxious to meet each other.

Elizabeth and I took an early train to the city on Saturday. Nick met us at the train station and wanted to take us to breakfast, but Elizabeth and I had already eaten, so we joined Nick for a coffee. Nick's driver was waiting for us and drove us to the Auto Shop. We were so impressed with Nick's first legitimate business venture. It was so high tech and elaborate for an Auto Repair Shop. We admired the high priced European cars.

"How did you ever think of having all the detail you have here?" I asked.

"Just by being aware and exposed will broaden any aspect of your life," Nick said.

We were soon whisked away to the museum where Felicia worked. She was there to greet us and was so excited about finally meeting Elizabeth.

"Normally, I would have someone here to show you around, but there is no one better than Nick."

I had to ask, "How in the world did you ever learn as much as this?"

Nick just laughed and said, "That's another story—maybe someday I'll tell you."

We met Felicia when the museum closed. We walked through the streets, did some shopping, and finally stopped for dinner.

Nick said, "Look at our two women in front of us. They haven't stopped talking since they met. It's as though they've known each other all their lives."

I replied, "I'm still trying to adjust to this wonderful life."

"You'll do just fine. You're a survivor, and I know you can handle any situation that comes up," said Nick. We took the train home after lots of hugs and promises to get together again real soon.

Within a few days, I was contacted by the CIA with instructions to report to the Army Base for four days for a preliminary briefing.

That night, I told Elizabeth that I had an opportunity to work for the Government. I wanted to check out all my options before I made up my mind, but I thought it was something that I'd like to do.

"What would you be doing for the Government?"

"Well, that's what I'm going to find out. I know it will be a high security position, so I may not be able to tell you everything, but I will always let you know as much as I can. Just for now, do not say anything to anyone about this."

"Whatever will make you happy is what you should do," Elizabeth said, "as long as you're careful."

CHAPTER 17

Malcolm reached John by phone to tell him he would meet him at the base. It was always good for John to hear Malcolm's voice, and he looked forward to seeing his friend again.

A few days later, I said good-bye to my family and to Elizabeth and headed to the base by train. I saw Malcolm right away and we embraced. As usual, I was engulfed by his largeness. I felt I was being bent in half when Malcolm hugged me. We were taken to our quarters, along with six other men, and Malcolm and I were assigned to the same room. We had 45 minutes to do whatever we needed and to then show up at Building B for our first meeting. Three strong-looking men in dark suits briefed us on the next four days.

We were to learn what to look for in a crowd, as well as to listen to sounds we were unaware of in the past. They would train our eyes to remember detail and almost develop a sixth sense. We would be shown how to use our weapons at great distances and up close. We were also to learn about makeup and disguises with facial hair and hairpieces. This was our four day briefing of what the later training would entail. By the end of the four days, you would know if you wanted to make this commitment.

*   *   *   *

Malcolm and I returned to my home, as he was spending a few days with me before going back to Detroit. Elizabeth didn't know what day I was returning, so Malcolm and I went to the card shop to surprise her late in the afternoon. As we came close to the shop, we saw police cars, an ambulance, and a crowd of people. My heart raced, and I shouted to a guy from the neighborhood: "What the hell's going on? What happened?"

"Oh my God, John, Elizabeth was held up and she's hurt. I don't know, gunshot, wounded, or what. That's all I know."

Malcolm and I pushed our way through the small crowd of people until we were stopped by a cop. The cop said, "You can't go any further than this." Malcolm grabbed me by the arm and shoved us past the cops. Malcolm pushed into the card shop and saw Elizabeth lying in a pool of blood. Crime scene people were all over the place, and he realized she was dead.

"Oh my God, John...." Malcolm grabbed me and saw a glazed, stone cold look on my face.

I said, "We have to get back to home base and regroup."

Malcolm said, "Do you know where you are?"

"Yes, we're in enemy territory, and one of our own is down, so I'm going back. You stay here and get all the information you can."

Malcolm said, "John ..."

"No, Malcolm, this is the way it has to be. Come back to camp when you're finished."

I went right to the garage at my house where I had left my knife and some old clothes from gardening, and put on my old boots. I waited very patiently for Malcolm to arrive. It was getting dark, and I heard a familiar sound, telling me that Malcolm was there. I answered in the same sound and let Malcolm into the garage through the back door.

"What did you find out?"

"It was three black kids who were seen running out of the store, a little description of them is all I have. Sit down and we'll talk about it."

"Okay, Malcolm, go ahead." I stood up slowly and said, "All the training we've had; now we will put it to the test. Who thought we would be using it for ourselves. I know I don't even have to ask this, but are you in this with me?"

Malcolm responded by giving me a warm hug.

We left the garage together, with Malcolm going to the local black clubs and bars to see what he could get.

I gave him money from my pocket, "Here. Buy lots of drinks. Get people to loosen up. I'm gonna be on the streets."

We split up to go our own ways, planning to meet around 2:30 a.m., behind St. Michael's Church. When we met, neither of us had gotten any information at all.

I told Malcolm, "Go to sleep in my garage and talk to my parents. Tell them I am sane and okay. I can't even see my mother right now. I first need to be alone. I want you to keep in touch with them for me. Let's hook up tomorrow, after dark, at the church."

I was anxious to resume my search through the city where the junkies, the winos, and the derelicts wandered around.

Malcolm got up early the next morning and knocked on my back door. My mother and grandmother were in the kitchen, very upset about everything that had happened and over not knowing where I was.

Malcolm was hugged with: "Where's my Johnny? Where's my Johnny?"

"All I can tell you is that John is okay. He's doing what he has to. I'm looking out for him. He'll be fine.

Mother asked, "Do you want some breakfast?"

"I'd love some," Malcolm said.

Mother continued with, "Nick called me and told me that he knew you were here. He knows that John is not communicating with anyone. Nick wants you to call him at this number."

Malcolm asked to use the phone and dialed the number.

Nick told Malcolm, "I know what Johnny's going through. He won't listen to anything anybody has to say right now. He has to do what he has to do. I know you're with him, and I want you to protect and help him. I have people on the street also that are watching John. We'll stay in touch. I'll make arrangements for you both to disappear."

Malcolm went back to the garage to lie down and take a nap. He had gotten very little sleep and he knew there was not much he could do during daylight hours.

I slept in an alley that night. I woke up to find a priest and a few street people with me. The priest handed me a cup of hot coffee and asked me why I was on the street.

"Do you know what you're doing? I'll tell you where to go to get a good meal."

I first nodded my head in response, not wanting to talk to anybody. My mind was focused on doing what I knew I had to do. The priest led me by the arm.

"Let's get a decent meal and bathroom."

I was led willingly. I spent the rest of the day talking to homeless people. I brought a six-pack of beer to give out to people as I started conversations about the girl that got robbed and stabbed in the card shop, but nobody I was in contact with even knew about it.

In late afternoon, I stopped to buy a newspaper, and the priest showed up again. He greeted me and asked me to join him in a second hot meal of the day. I questioned the priest about the robbery and the stabbing. The priest told me he read about it in the paper.

"There are three black young men the police are looking for. Most likely, these three kids are from the south end and they probably would hang out at the Golden Gate or Club One."

I was so happy to hear these words, but hardly responded. It was the first and only lead I had. I finished my meal, and it was just turning dusk. The priest asked if I had a place to sleep, but I said I was taken care of.

"Here's a few dollars in case you need it."

I walked, looking for the area the priest had told me about. I searched for the bars so I would know them in the dark. I went back to the church to wait for Malcolm to give him the news. Malcolm showed up after dark, and I told him what I had learned.

For the next several nights, Malcolm spent his time at the clubs with the locals. He put out the word that he had a job to do and needed a few guys to help him out.

"I would like to have guys like the ones that did the card shop job. If I could find guys like that, they could make some serious money; not this nickel and dime stuff."

A couple of nights went by, and then a guy approached Malcolm and said to him, "Why are you here asking for guys to do a job for you and asking about the card shop job? What are you, a cop?

Malcolm laughed at that, "No fucking way. I'm so far from being a cop. Believe me."

"Well then, why do you need guys like the ones who did the card shop?"

"The job I have planned to do has people involved, and if anything slips up, there can be no hesitation to kill."

"What kind of a job is it?"

"It has to do with a jewelry store during daylight hours ... when all of the good stuff is out, and not in the safe. There are three women and a guy that run the store. It would be quiet, grab, and run. I need guys with no guns, so no noise, but good knives in case anything goes wrong. No hesitation to steal and kill."

"What if I can get you these three guys?"

"Meet me here tomorrow night."

Malcolm once again met up with me at the back of the church. I had already been waiting for a while.

"I don't know if this is going to work. I keep running into dead ends and getting discouraged," I said.

Malcolm said, "I believe we're just beginning to get a little lucky. I talked with a guy who is going to hook me up with the guys who did the card shop. Tomorrow night, I'm gonna be asking these guys certain questions about the job, and I'll see to verify it with Nick. I'll never let you know the specifics of how Elizabeth died or what they did to her. But, I will let you know if we have the right guys or not. Nick will be able to get all the information through his connections with the police."

The next night, Malcolm went early to the Golden Gate to check out the place and got a table facing the bar and the front door, with his back to the wall. He ordered a bite to eat and a beer. An hour went by, and finally the guy from the night before came in and sat down at the table with him. He asked Malcolm to open his jacket and his shirt to see if he was wired. As Malcolm was taking off his jacket, he said, "Pat me down; believe me, I am not a cop." The guy patted his back and went down his legs.

Malcolm asked him if he wanted something to drink, and the guy said, "Yeah, I'll have a beer."

"Are the three guys gonna show up tonight?"

"Well, I'm one of them, and the other two are sitting at the bar."

He waved to the guys at the bar to come over. Malcolm said, "I have to ask you a couple of questions. Give me some details that only the guys who did the job would know about the robbery/murder, because they're the guys that I want to do this job for me."

Malcolm kept ordering rounds of shots and beers, and the men were becoming more and more comfortable. They started telling Malcolm about the job and how easy it was. It was a real rush to them.

Malcolm said, "The job that I want you to help me out with will get you a lot more money than what you made at the card shop. Give me a couple more days to get things set up, and I will meet you back here Friday night to go over the details."

Malcolm called Nick the next day to fill him in on what was happening and told him the graphic details of the murder and robbery. Nick made a few phone calls to those in the police department, to verify the same. Malcolm called Nick again the following day, and Nick asked how I was doing. Nick said everything pointed to the three guys; he was 100% sure. Nick told Malcolm he needed a day's notice to make arrangements for getting Malcolm and me out of town.

"Give me six hours' notice and a location before you do what has to be done. I know you and John are highly trained assassins," Nick said, "so I won't offer any assistance on what has to be done."

Malcolm met up with me. I was straining to learn more and losing my patience. "Keep your cool now; we will do what needs to be done," Malcolm assured me.

On that weekend, Malcolm met up with the three thugs at the bar and started buying drinks to continue to bond with these guys. They were getting antsy and excited about when they would do the job. Malcolm asked them a few more questions on how they did the card shop job. Not too much, as he didn't want to cause any suspicions.

The plan was for Sunday night, to meet in front of the club at 1:30 a.m.

"We'll go by the jewelry store, back door, and go over the layout."

Malcolm bought another round of drinks and then left. His last words were: "Don't tell nobody about any of this, our meeting Sunday night, or the heist, or it will be blown."

"We haven't opened our mouths to anybody. Nobody but us knows about it."

Malcolm called Nick Saturday morning to re-confirm the details of the murder of Elizabeth. He told Nick about the setup for Sunday night and gave him the location.

Nick said, "We'll see you then. Good luck. Be careful and be quiet."

After talking with Nick, Malcolm went to the soup kitchen, looking for me, figuring I would be there around lunchtime. The hall was busy, and he looked around and found me eating with the priest. Malcolm came up to me and said, "I hafta talk to you now."

I introduced Malcolm to the priest and we left together.

Malcolm told me everything was set up for Sunday night. "Meet me at the news stand on the corner of Dixwell and Wright. I'll be going into the alley with the guys around 1:50 a.m. Be there and sit in front of the alleyway, looking like you're drunk, and we'll walk right by you."

Malcolm explained: "I'll be in the middle of them, two on one side of me and one on the other. You grab the one, and I'll grab the two, and we go from there."

Sunday night finally came, and Malcolm met the three young guys. As they were walking a couple of blocks, Malcolm said, "I'll take you down the alley to get to the back door of the jewelry store."

As they went into the alleyway, Malcolm could see me huddled against the wall with my knees up and my head hanging, looking every bit the part of a wino.

Twenty feet into the alley, I came up behind my target and slit his throat in a split second. Malcolm, with his big hands, grabbed the other two by their throats, freezing them in their tracks. Then, I grabbed one from behind, and as I was slitting his throat, Malcolm had already killed the third, saying: "This is for the beautiful young girl whose life you destroyed."

I fell to my knees, hysterical, as Malcolm hung the three guys by their feet upside down from the fire escape. Malcolm picked me up and told me to hold on a little bit longer.

It took just seconds from start to finish. We quickly surveyed the area to make sure we didn't leave anything behind. All was silent. Sunday night is the quietest night of the week.

We left the alley and walked to the location that Malcolm had planned with Nick. A car was waiting there with Nick in the passenger seat. The driver looked very familiar, even though he didn't have his white collar on.

Malcolm urged me, "Let it all out now. You haven't given yourself the chance to mourn for Elizabeth. The hatred can't consume you for life."

Nick turned to the back and told Malcolm, "I have everything arranged for you both to disappear until things cool down. The government's offer isn't going anywhere; they were well informed as to what transpired. Those who love you have been reassured that you are okay, but you must do what you are doing. Don't worry. Give it time."

THE END

978-0-595-42464-
0-595-42464-3

Printed in the United States
200794BV00003B/1-30/A

9 780595 424641